LET ME DIE A WOMAN

Alan Kelly

Pulp Press

For more information please visit
www.pulppress.co.uk
www.myspace.com/pulppress
or email **answers@pulppress.co.uk**

First published in Great Britain by Pulp Press

All paper used in the printing of this book has been made
from wood grown in managed, sustainable forests.

ISBN13: 978-1-907499-39-5
Printed and bound in the UK
Pulp Press is an imprint of Indepenpress Publishing Limited
25 Eastern Place
Brighton
BN2 1GJ

A catalogue record of this book is available from
the British Library
Cover design by Alex Young
www.brainofalexyoung.com

Acknowledgments

First I would like to thank the following for their support: Danny and Kim and everyone at Pulp Press, Alex Young for the fanfuck-ingtastic cover. Cathi Unsworth has been a rock this last year. Susan Tomaselli and everyone at 3:AM. The book is dedicated to Heidi Martinuzzi, Shannon Lark, Hannah Neurotica, Elvira, Jovanka Vuckovic, Suzi Lorraine & women in horror everywhere. The following people who have never let me down are: Tiffany Fitzgerald Brosnan, Luke and Jon, Gina and Audrey, Vincent & Catherine, my future husband Matthew Solis, Carmel Kinsella, Sharon Fitzgerald, Kenneth Scare, Noel and Katryna, Margaret, Declan, Thomas and Tina Esmonde. Ita and Stan Kettle, Billy and Maura (Fred and Rose), James and Caroline, Rose and Jimmy Keogh, Polish Greg for making me long island ice-teas in Panti Bar, Nanny Lil and my mother, and Amy Tarr - the first person to have faith in me!

1
When the Old World Was Good

Jessica Spark sat on the edge of the bed and waited for her mother to fill a basket with food for the 'Scarecrow Festival' in Roundwood later that afternoon. She surveyed herself in the full-length mirror of her sister's bedroom and sighed. She was almost twenty-three now, another boyfriend had broken up with her, her drinking the cause this time. She knew she withdrew from others; she didn't need Sally Jessie to tell her that. This time Jessica hadn't even given him the chance not to be an asshole. It was a cycle she had tried and failed to break. She turned on someone before they got the opportunity to turn on her.

Jessica frowned at the mirror and noticed her sister's Pekingese Shaggy, a vibrating ball of twitchy fur, watching from the doorway. *It was her mother Lila's fault she drank*, she thought. It was Lila's fault she could never keep a man and, instead, lost herself in chance encounter after chance encounter. But, Jessica could live with the scars Lila caused. Caused by withdrawing her affection when she was just a girl.

Satisfied, Jessica dabbed on some blue eye shadow, let her vamp red hair fall either side of her narrow face and blew her reflection a kiss. On her way out she levelled her gaze with Shaggy as if to mesmerise him and, when he was distracted, she kicked the poor dog out of her way and chuckled all the way down the stairs.

Sparking a cigarette Jessica watched her mother place pickled gherkins and spray cheese into the hamper. One of Lila's mingy stray cats was licking itself at Jessica's feet, a furry leg raised high in the air. She pushed it away from her with the toe of her boot.

'You goin' to help or what or just sit there smoking your life away?' Lila asked, clucking about the kitchen.

Jessica ignored her and took a long drag on her cigarette. Why should she help? It was her mother's idea to go to this festival, not her's.

Lila's wizened face looked at her with carefully restrained fury.

'I'm depressed,' Jessica muttered under her breath.

Lila rolled her eyes and threw her pipe thin arms in the air. Jessica held a delicate hand over her own eyes and pretended to notice something interesting at her feet. Jessica despaired that the older women got, the more incessantly they jabbered on and the more convinced they were that they were right about everything. Or maybe that was just her mother? She doubted it. Sitting there watching the Wicked Witch Jessica realised that the mother-daughter relationship was the most brutal relationship of them all. She decided, as she stubbed out her fag in a used eggcup, that she was never going to give birth.

'Come on, come on,' Lila demanded, pinching at Jessica's arms. Jessica swatted her away and grabbed the basket while Lila rang to confirm the taxi was on its way and would be parked at their gate in five minutes. She pressed two bottles of Cava into the bottom of the basket, out of sight under the jammy dodgers and the portable radio. The day might go to plan after all, she smiled. As she locked the kitchen window she couldn't help another chuckle. The cats wouldn't get anywhere near the spread her mother had laid out for them. Jessica decided that, after today, she would call the RSPCA and have the animals removed while her mother was at her 'Adult Literacy' class on Monday.

Out on the porch a single Magpie flew straight by her. She hated them. Those bastards had a way of flying straight into your vision and waving their fucking little tails mockingly so that you couldn't not notice them. Jessica saluted it and looked around her mother's overgrown garden for something purple to touch. There were some flowers Lila had planted in the spring and she ripped them from their stems viciously.

'Bastard Magpies,' she seethed.

Jessica felt her phone vibrate in her back pocket and knew without looking who was sending the message. It was Ron. Who else? It was the fifteenth message she'd received since she dumped him last Saturday (or rather, he dumped her). Maybe she should plot a move somewhere, get a job as a hostess in a club in Ibiza? She was young, beautiful, had no trouble mimicking intelligence, why not?

Jessica got into the back of the car and pushed the basket over to the other side. She was beginning to think, as they pulled off, that he could cause her some real hassle. She'd had stalkers before and it was fucking horrible. She had been around the block in this situation already. Try not to have anymore contact with him – which was not easy in a small place – but maybe she was being melodramatic? After all these kind of people thrived on attention and if she didn't give him any, well, eventually he'd go away. Satisfied with her own problem solving she relaxed.

Her mother was playing Snowy White's *Bird of Paradise* on the portable radio and Jessica watched the road lead away from the battered two-story she shared with Lila. They passed through the village where a group of boys were gathered, rolling joints and drinking cider with ice outside the local pub. The taxi took a sharp turn onto the Arklow Road and she caught her mother squinting into the rear view mirror. God she really didn't age well. Her face, which perhaps was once pretty, was now hard-bitten by a desperate sort of need. *Lila had done everything for her sisters*, thought Jessica. She wished that just once, only once, Lila could allow herself to smile.

Jessica was enjoying this music, grateful that the driver wouldn't get the opportunity to listen to the bland shite churned out on the hour, every hour by the local radio stations. This was the first time Jessica and Lila had spent an entire day together in a while, and she was determined that it would be her last. At least around here, in the countryside.

Jessica dreamed about her escape route as they passed Glenealy, another cul-de-sac with a closed down train station, one pub and a slaughterhouse. Yes, Jessica couldn't stay here and stay sane. After the festival she would sit her mother down and explain that she needed to leave for London. She needed the relative freedom and the anonymity of the city. She needed to get lost and be whoever the fuck she wanted to be.

Today she was on her way to Roundwood, a nice little patch for inbreeding, with no real incomers since the Vikings. Why did her mother even suggest a scarecrow festival anyway? Jessica had never seen a scarecrow, let alone an entire army of them. The extent of her experience with them was being forced to watch the nauseating *Wizard of OZ*. That character was a simple-minded idiot with, she suspected, paedophilic inclinations what with the way he was fawning all over Dorothy and that Godforsaken mutt Toto who always followed the prize fools around. Jessica had always preferred the witch. At least she had some spunk.

Jessica lit a cigarette and was about to take a drag when her mother ripped it from her mouth.

'Not now Jess,' she hissed, rolling the window down and throwing it out into the nearest ditch. Jessica would've slapped her but such a move wouldn't have been very wise with a witness present. She returned her eyes to the window. The cab continued to drive further inland, they passed a lake, some roads with a dusty lane of cottages and some pheasants that ran out onto the lane then scarpered when they heard the car engine. Jessica pulled the window down, liking the smack of the wind on her face, the music in her ears and the sun in her eyes. She deserved all this, she smiled into the heat, it was bliss.

Jessica still wanted a drink though. She decided there and then that she'd be honest and ask her mother to open a bottle which they could share. She started a sentence but it was snatched from her lips by the wind and scattered on the road behind her. *Fuck, I'll have to do it myself*, she thought. She reached over and carefully removed a Cava and a corkscrew from the basket. Jessica caught a disapproving glance from her mother and threw her back a sardonic smile.

'Cheers Queers,' she said, holding up the bottle and offering a salute, and then taking a long swig of the drink. It was a light bodied refreshing Cava with barely any alcohol and it hit the spot. Her mother looked back at her and her face was torn between concern and disgust.

'Jessica what have I ever done to you? I thought you wanted to come with me?' Jessica took another mouthful of the Cava before replying.

'It's a drink on a day out mother, that's all. Now could you not worry about me? I'm a big girl and I can take care of myself,' she said. When her mother frowned Jessica thought that the lines were so deep that a farmer could probably sow potatoes in her forehead but she also thought better of vocalising the image. Lila smiled at the taxi driver and applied some lipstick in the mirror, never taking her eyes off either Jessica or the bottle. After she had freshened up she asked in a much calmer voice, 'are you unhappy, I mean really unhappy?' The heat was stifling and Jessica had already polished off the entire bottle.

'Not unhappy exactly,' replied Jessica, closing her eyes and leaning her head back on the headrest. When she closed her eyes, she saw violent images of Ron, in a bathtub, slowly sinking down into dirty water under a film of coagulated brownish gore. She opened them again quickly and asked the driver how much further until they reached the festival.

Her mother's hands were buried in the basket for a while and eventually she took out a bottle of water.

'It's warm Jess, but it should be OK' she smiled sadly, handing the bottle over. Jessica muttered her thanks and took long hungry gulps of the water, which rinsed her mouth of the tepid taste of cheap wine. She sloshed it around and spat it out of the open window.

'Charmed, I'm sure!' Lila said to the taxi driver, who laughed. Jessica sat quietly while they came into Roundwood. The entire village was decorated with lines of flags, stalls full of various knick knacks, leery men drinking lager and young couples shouting at their babies. There were scarecrows everywhere. Their button eyes and jaunty hats could be seen peering over walls, from behind the tents where the stalls were, looking around corners.

'Scarecrows everywhere but where they want to be.' whispered Jessica to herself while peering from the car. The taxi driver turned to Jessica.

'You women be careful where you wander today OK?'

'Why?' asked Lila, fixing her skirt.

He took a deep breath.

'You've not heard about the incidents then girls?'

'What incidents would they be?' asked Jessica.

'Well,' the driver began, 'horse and cow ripping goin' on lately.'

'What on earth is horse and cow ripping?' Jessica asked, feeling a bit annoyed.

'Someone or *somethin'* goin' into the fields, cutting great holes out of the animals, plucking their eyes out, cutting off their sex organs, that sorta thing.'

Jessica's mother had gone pale, her brow knitted with worry. Jessica threw twenty euro at the cab driver and shouted sarcastically, 'thanks for the tale dickhead,' before slamming the car door.

Jessica looked at Lila, who suddenly seemed really nervy. Feeling a bit jittery herself she wrapped her arms around her.

'Don't listen to him, the idiot was just talking about a scene from *Deliverance* or something,'

Jessica linked arms with her mother across the square, quietly pleased that this was only a bridge that had to be crossed in order to get out of her situation.

Just thinking about what had allegedly happened to those animals brought on nausea in Jessica and she wondered what sort of person would do such a thing. It had to be a few people at least, to subdue animals that large. Jessica watched the people moving around her, she felt so very lost here. She thought of the lyrics from a Tom Waits song Ron, her ex boyfriend, used to make her listen to. It was the one about putting a pocket full of flowers on her grave, in a time when the old world was good. The dreadful people in this place were the flowers and the pocket was this small village in the middle of nowhere, a lost old shantytown in time.

She saw a pub up ahead and felt like sitting outside and having a drink.

'Come on Mom, I want a drink.' Her mother made a choked sound like an animal caught in a snare but Jessica dragged her on towards the pub anyway. It was apparently the highest pub in Ireland, or so she'd read in some tourist brochure years ago. Inside it was heaving and she was forced to elbow her way to the bar while Lila waited in the beer garden outside.

'Excuse me, can I…' Jessica shouted and the barman ignored her, serving the hard faced cow beside her with vicious peroxide hair, hoop earrings and the tattoos to complete her ensemble.

'I was first alright?' the woman scowled at her.

If looks could kill, thought Jessica, *the undertakers would be throwing her skinny little body in the ground.* She felt like giving the dog a lashing with her venomous tongue and, any other time, she would have but her mother was waiting for her and the last thing she needed was a bar brawl with some ugly skank. Jessica tried to get the barman's attention three more times when a voice behind her said, 'you're not a local, huh?'

She turned around and was knocked for six by the vision in front of her. A beautiful man, dressed entirely in black with the greenest eyes and smooth, sallow skin hovered over her.

'No, I'm not, thank God,' replied Jessica, eyeballing the bitch at the bar. He carefully parted and wet his lips with his tongue and Jessica felt her cunt hammering between her legs.

'What'll it be then?' he gestured towards the bar.

'A double vodka and tonic and an orange juice.'

Jessica took some money from her purse and was going to hand it over to him but he was already at the bar. While she was waiting she noticed that the skank and a group of her friends were watching her from their corner of the pub. Jessica stared back at them defiantly. She wouldn't be intimidated by a small group of village girls. She almost felt sorry for them, with their pockmarked skin, greasy ponytails and yellow teeth. They'd no doubt have a bunch of neglected, dragged up bastards stored away somewhere so they could drink their social welfare cheques.

Jessica also noticed a gaggle of rugby player types eyeing her, for obvious reasons, and she undid two of the buttons on her fitted jumper. One of the girls got up from her seat and walked towards her. She was a towering brute of a woman with frizzy red hair and she looked like she'd have no problem cracking your face open. She stood looking down on Jessica, who ignored her.

'Ya gotta problem or something?' the hulk barked down at her.

'No,' began Jessica, 'other than your BO, I'm quite alright. Now why don't you do everyone a favour and go home and feed your horses, pig tits.'

'I ought to smear your face over the wall, cunt.'

Jessica turned her back on Red, not wanting to be a part of a tedious debacle. But Red had other ideas. She lunged for Jessica, grabbing her hair and flooring her. Another girl joined in and kicked Jessica hard in the stomach. Jessica bit down hard on Red's free hand and she let go of her hair. She got to her feet and, without thinking, head butted Red hard in the face. Jessica felt a crack and Red backed onto a table where a family were eating, her nose pouring thick blood. Jessica looked sharply at Red's weasel faced mate.

'Come on bitch,' hissed Jessica.

The weasel started apologising profusely and the stranger in black materialised beside her, his jaw hanging. Jessica took the drink from him, knocked it back with one shot and handed him the empty glass.

'What the fuck happened?' he asked.

'She,' said Jessica, pointing at Red and her cronies, 'started something that I finished.'

She went to the bar and ordered the same again and the barman didn't dare ignore her this time.

'Where did you get to Jess?' her mother asked, when she brought the drinks out to the beer garden. Lila looked at the man beside Jessica and the tiniest smile was promised by the movements of her mouth, but denied at the last second.

'Mom this is…' Jessica was about to introduce her compatriot when she realised she didn't know his name.

He picked up on this quickly and finished her sentence.

'I'm Benjamin and you are?' he replied.

'Lila and this is my daughter Jessica. Nice to meet you.'

Jessica had never seen her mother come over all girlish. It was sickening.

'He knows my name Mother,' Jessica told her.

They sat watching the old farmers in battered tractors hauling hay bails back to the harvested fields. Children played with water guns, people ate candy floss and hotdogs and bought cut-price clothes from market stalls. Her mother was like the Spanish Inquisition with Benjamin, firing question after question at him. If Jessica hadn't been so pleasantly numb from the vodka she'd have felt embarrassed. She turned to Benjamin and asked if there was accommodation anywhere in Roundwood.

'Ah yeah, The Coach House does it, though it could be fully booked with the festival,' he said.

'Yes but there is an Tocher House on the main street too,' Lila interrupted.

Jessica caught something in the corner of her eye but when she turned around all she saw was a pebble dashed wall. She thought she caught a glimpse of someone, or something peering around a corner at her. It was only brief and could have been her imagination but she swore to herself that she saw a pair of cold, button eyes being fixed on her.

'Did you see something just now,' asked Jessica, pointing at the wall.

Her mother and Benjamin were engrossed in a discussion on matters horticultural and both stopped to stare at her with almost identical expressions of bemusement.

'No, we didn't' Benjamin shrugged, and her mother gave her another one of those patronising stares that seemed to say 'haven't you drank enough for one day young lady?'

'Fine, I'm gonna go walk the vodka off, see you later'.

Benjamin offered to join her but Jessica waved him away, making some excuse about wanting space.

From the main street she could see the Vartry Lakes glisten in the heat. The village was extremely remote, surrounded by hills and forests. There was a camping site nearby called Glenmalure, a place Jessica had gone when she was younger, with her father. She walked out of the village. Everywhere her eyes wandered there was a Godforsaken scarecrow. She stopped in front of one. It wore a bright orange hat and an oily crombie. Its mouth was stitched into a smile on a threadbare sack. The very idea of scarecrows gave her the jitters; being stuck in a field all day, completely alone, never having anybody to talk to, only vicious taunting birds for company.

Jessica leaned over and planted a light kiss on the scarecrows cheek. When she did, she hurled. The stench emanating from it was that of rotting meat; a corpse left too long in the sun. She doubled over on the path and threw her guts up. Leaning against the wall with one arm, she dry heaved until there was nothing left inside her. When she eventually got herself together she looked up to see the spires of *The Church of Lawrence of Toole*; a jagged black line cutting into the orange sun.

She bought some water and sipped it as she made her way back to the pub. Why would anyone put rotting meat inside a scarecrow anyway? Unless it was to do with the cow slaughter. Even though she was drunk and fucked off at everything, this was something she couldn't quite get a grip on. She could throttle her mother for bringing her all the way out here. She'd stick it out for the time being though. It wouldn't be much longer until she was on a plane and away from her mother and all this.

Jessica turned a corner to see Red and her cronies waiting for her. Red had a swollen nose and two black eyes. Jessica folded her arms and smirked. When would people learn she was nobody's victim, least of all a fat ugly ginger minger like Red? If Jessica had to, she was more than prepared to mash Red's face down the nearest drain and had no qualms about cracking her cronies' ankles.

'I've no time for this shit,' Jessica said slowly, barely veiling the menace in her voice.

'We're gonna kick the shit out of ya,' shouted Red, brandishing a rolling pin. Her weasels laughed behind her.

Jessica made an attempt to pass but her way was blocked. Red lifted her arm in the air and was about to bring the rolling pin down on Jessica's head when a scream cut through the air. Red and Jessica turned to see that a scarecrow had hold of one of the cronies and was very slowly peeling back her scalp. The girl was making similar noises to a small animal being slowly eaten by a cat.

Red dropped her rolling pin and looked at her friend. Jessica picked it up and, when Red got distracted by another one of her crony's pathetic screams, Jessica took a swing and smashed the rolling pin into her kneecap. Red screamed in agony and Jessica could soon see hot tears and bloody snot running down her face.

Jessica moved carefully past the scarecrow, which had now gripped the girls tongue and was in the process of tearing it from her head. Jessica ran along the main street. Everywhere scarecrows were animated and there was no prejudice in the choice of people they attacked. A husband and wife were being slowly flayed alive by two miniature scarecrows while others were gouging out eyeballs and stringing up children, only to disembowel them with scythes. It wasn't long before a few of them locked eyes on Jessica.

Jessica looked around for some sort of weapon and, seeing a pickaxe, grabbed hold of it. A scarecrow was moving at her with surprising speed. She swung the pick, decapitating the creature. A shower of maggots and slimy meat rained down on her. She ran back to the pub in search of her mother and Benjamin and went inside, grateful for the coolness from the heat. Everyone seemed so still, until it dawned on her that everyone was dead or, at the very least, getting there. She saw an entire family with their mouths stitched shut, buttons where their eyes should be and vicious fatal wounds from their groins to their gullets. Where the hell were her mother and Benjamin? She took the back door into the beer garden and was greeted by even more carnage. Jessica held her hand over her mouth and began to cry.

'Mother,' she called quietly. 'It's Jess, mother.'

She sat down on a chair that was covered in blood and hugged the pickaxe to her. She could still feel all those cold eyes fixed on her and she held her hand to her chest to prevent herself from being sucked down into a whirlpool of paranoia. She sat for almost an hour among the dead, pretending not to hear the footsteps slowly stealing up on her.

Jessica waited until the last second, until a hand touched her shoulder, then swung around with a ferocity she didn't know she was capable of and buried the pickaxe into the scarecrows head. Blood momentarily blinded her, but once she had wiped her vision back into focus she saw it hadn't been a scarecrow, but Lila. She had killed her own mother. She killed her mother. Lila lay thrashing about at her feet and Jessica wept.

She heard a crash inside the pub and Benjamin came out, unharmed. He looked at Jessica and then at the body at her feet.

'What has happened?' he asked, his voice oddly calm with no underscore of the panic that this situation should invariably cause.

'I killed my mother,' replied Jessica. 'It was an accident.'

Benjamin approached her, his arms held out in front of him. Jessica was covered in gore, maggots and her mother's blood. Benjamin was getting closer; Jessica leaned down quickly and pulled the pickaxe out of her mother's face.

'Don't come any closer fucker.' Said Jessica, holding the pickaxe in front of her.

Benjamin stopped a few feet short of where Jessica stood.

'Calm down Jess. This is only a game the village plays every year. It's all a charade. Really. Trust me.'

Jessica wondered what he meant by charade. Scarecrows were a charade but the slaughter wasn't.

'Interesting choice of words Benji.'

She took a few steps back and nearly slipped in her mother's blood. Benjamin took some careful steps towards her; his movements looked mechanical as if something was controlling him.

'Us, we, the 'scarecrows' grow weary of being made to stand all day in fields. Do you know what it's like to be stuck Jessica?'

His words struck a chord with her but she wasn't going to give him the satisfaction of letting him know that.

'Of course, doesn't everybody?' she shouted, swinging the pickaxe at him.

She missed, but at least it gave her some time. She turned and jumped onto a table that was set right by the wall that encircled the pub. She threw the pickaxe over and managed to crawl over after it. When she landed on the grass pain shot up through her leg and she stumbled onto the ground. Jessica pushed herself up onto all fours. When she smelt the rot she turned quickly and a bag was thrown over her head. The smell was unbearable and she soon lost consciousness.

Peering over walls, their eyes follow you around corners…

The pain in her wrists burned and her tongue felt like it had been left out in the sun and had begun to sprout hair. When she opened her eyes, her hands and legs were tied tightly to a wheel. She was in a barn and surrounded by scarecrows. They looked down on her with their button eyes. She struggled but there was no point; she was caught and at their mercy. Every time she moved the ropes burned into her wrists. She tried screaming but it came out as a muffled croak.

'You're stuck Jessica,' said a voice from somewhere.

She recognised it as Benjamin's. The scarecrows parted and he stood at her feet. He was naked and smiling and his skin had black thread running through it. Beneath it looked like the meat had been stacked haphazardly in there.

'What are you?' asked Jessica.

Slowly Benjamin pulled the pieces of chords from his stomach and began to part the flesh. Jessica felt sick rising in her throat. A goat and a lambs head were pushed together where his lungs should be. Jessica screamed when she looked closer and saw that the animals' mouths and eyes still moved around frantically.

'There is no point screaming Jessica. No point at all. We've been using animal parts so far…' he let his voice trail off, so Jessica could fill in the blanks.

No, they couldn't use her? She looked back at him. In the centre of his chest she could make out a small reptilian creature moving through the dead meat. She thought it looked over at her.

'We weren't strong so we used the animals, but people will be better. We can use the whole of them, to live,' Benjamin whispered.

'And what about us? What happens to us?' replied Jessica.

'You'll still be in there. There is no point in destroying you,' he said.

'Why did you kill everybody then?' Jessica screamed at him.

'My scarecrows got carried away. Those people are just meat now, but we have you Jessica,' he smiled.

'Me?' mumbled Jessica.

'We want you to join us, travel the world, find others and indoctrinate them,' said Benjamin.

Jessica tried to digest what he was telling her. She wanted to scream again, and kick and thrash but that would be pointless.

'I agree,' gasped Jessica, finally.

'Oh Jessica, first things first,' Benjamin laughed over his shoulder as he left the barn.

Four scarecrows stood on either side of the wheel; one of them was holding a large black jar. Carefully it removed the lid and reached inside. Jessica gasped when she saw the thing it lifted out. It looked like a long purple catfish with razor spikes lining its back and a human baby face. Jessica screamed as a scarecrow, which looked like a huge corn dolly, came in dressed as a midwife. It opened and held her knees apart. Then she could feel something crawl up inside. Jessica screamed and screamed until blackness like she'd never known before pulled her under.

*

Three years later Jessica sat staring from a third floor coffee shop window on Grafton Street. It hadn't been so bad, these past few years. She'd left the festival and didn't ever return home; it was never really home anyway. She had seen Japan, Australia, India, and America and left her mark everywhere she went. She was reading that a clown festival was taking place in Phoenix Park and it was estimated that almost 5000 people were expected to show up in fancy dress. She closed the paper, smiled and stared down at the street below. This was only the beginning.

'It's harvest time…'

2
Kill Fee

This is a *discipline and I am only hiding the fact that I am no celebrity journalist* thought Bunny Flask, gritting her teeth and tapping her fingernails on the ostentatious oval shaped marble desk across from the most sexist cunt in the publishing world: Mick Jones. It had started a month ago when he'd bought out *Blood Rag* magazine and demoted her from Deputy Editor to secretary. The problems began the moment he arrived, innocently enough. First he'd introduced error into her copy and, after that, it was all down-hill. When he hired a mediocre fanzine writer he was screwing to do her job she'd decided that this was about as much as she was prepared to take. She's asked the day before if he'd hold counsel with her and the motherfucker had hop, skipped and jumped at the chance.

The two years she'd worked there she'd worked hard, been relentlessly fucking cheery; sub-editing every other article, polishing copy for the amateur writers. She had taken this magazine out of the underground and put it on the top shelf. He'd already found her replacement. Some woman by

the name of Alice Fiend who'd only returned to Ireland having travelled the world and was now apparently 'very big'
in advertising, sales and radio. Alice Fiend had developed
a proposal for a new '*Blood Rag Radio*' show and both men
and women were lining up around the block to get a free
demo.

Bunny needed to leave Blood Rag after she realised the
editor was mad. A few days ago he had locked her in a room
and wouldn't allow her to come out until she had written one
hundred good reasons why she was lucky to have the job. She
kicked and screamed but he refused to open the door. While
she was at work writing her reasons and cursing the lardy bastard, the publisher rang her boyfriend and told him that his
girlfriend had a secret smack habit. Her boyfriend tried to finish their relationship the following day by text message.

So, Bunny sat there in Jones's office in her rah-rah skirt,
skin tight PVC trousers and Jean Paul Gaultier top, her pitch
black hair teased high on her head. It took all of Bunny's
strength to not say something to Fatboy, but she wanted
to deal with this with grace; a first for her. His piggy eyes
looked her up and down and she wished she'd worn a bra
under the semi-transparent top; his face looked like a block
of grotesque cheese left baking on a curb in Ballyfermot.
Bunny's eyes strayed to a ballpoint pen and she contem-
plated for a moment doing a *Nikita* and driving it into his
stubby little hand but stabbing the ugly fucker once wouldn't
be enough for her.

'Well, Ms Flask. Having looked over your one hundred
reasons, I've decided there is no longer a place for you at
Blood Rag,' Piggy began.

'You asshole. You're getting rid, just like you destroyed my relationship, 'cos I wouldn't suck your squirrel's dick' she spat, that ballpoint pen beginning to look more appealing with every passing second.

He'd locked her in a room against her will. She'd consult a tribunal, but then, there was her drug use. He could use that against her. This fat motherfucker had every bastard in the city in his pockets and she'd never be hired again. She decided the best option was to leave and request a kill fee later.

Bunny stormed out of the office furious, clacking down Grafton Street in her black cha cha heels. She felt anger flushing through her when she realised that this was one of those moments she would look back on and cry about which, if Piggy fat prick had his way, was going to be the high-light of her life when she looked back from her deathbed in a crappy one-bedroom shithole apartment in Ranleigh. She hadn't met her yet but she would confront this Alice Fiend and tell her exactly what she was getting herself into. Yes, she decided, she'd do exactly that. That was, once she'd had a stiff drink to calm herself down. She turned right and went into Bruxxels.

At the bar she ordered a shot of scotch without the rocks. She threw it back and ordered another. The bartender raised a bushy eyebrow and stared at her nipples.

'Anytime now would be a bonus cock,' said Bunny.

Mick Jones had fucked her over gradually; taken away all the power she had at Blood Rag so that she had ended up photocopying for the administrative staff. Part of the 'break-ing down process' was to ask her into his office, where he would throw all her features on the floor, saying how shit they were (features by Eli Roth, Debbie Rochon and Kiffany Boston-Gifford, amongst others).

Other days the fat daughter-fucker would routinely walk around an editorial meeting menacingly. The great big sweaty ball of sour horse-shit would waddle around the table telling each person individually they were pieces of shit and expendable, obviously seeking to cut their wages. These were damn good workers, earning 20,000 a year less than Fatboy spent annually having the crap sucked out of his ass or on Feng Shui. The final straw for Bunny was when he took her Bauhaus CDs out of the player and chucked them out the window.

Dwelling on it all was driving her around the bend. Oh yes, she'd get him and his new bitch Alice Fiend too. Bunny wanted that asshole dead. She wondered if that was wrong then smiled, ordered another scotch without the rocks and realised that, after all, there is nothing interesting about a healthy mind.

3
I'd Never Turn Down a Friend;
Hey I'd Never Turn Down a Stranger

Mick Jones watched the flame haired woman he'd come to know as Alice Fiend look out over the dusty, dirty city with a contempt that burned so furiously it nearly gave him the shits. She hated the *'little creatures'* and he knew exactly why. She had originally approached him on the pretext that there weren't enough women writing for Blood Rag. He assigned her a cover story on the independent film producer and exploitation guru Doris Wishman and she came back to him with a pretty impressive article, which he published verbatim. She'd come to him after that with the proposal to launch Blood Rag Radio. It would be advertised on the back pages of the magazine and she said it would *'infiltrate the heads of the little creatures'* which he liked.

Sales for Blood Rag had increased so much since her arrival he saw no reason not to agree to it. Blood Rag was selling over 60,000 units globally thanks to Alice Fiend's connections worldwide. It gave him the perfect excuse to get rid of Bunny Flask, the irritating little half-assed journalist with all her leftist bollocks about women in the horror genre. She'd nearly run the magazine into the ground during her ed-itrix-in-chief approach; championing guerrilla underground film-makers, soliciting obscure directors to write copy and giving his ex-wife Kiffany Boston-Gifford a monthly col-umn and making her the *'Blood Rag Beauty Queen'*.

Kiffany ran her own PR company and had shares in an American production and marketing company called *GUTS*. She wasn't a writer and she sure as shit knew sweet F all about the horror genre. Neither did that skinny little no tits, Bunny Flask for that matter.

When Mick discovered Alice's motives for joining Blood Rag and the real reason she wanted to begin a radio pro-gramme, he thought he'd strolled onto the set of an Ed Wood invasion movie, by which time, it was too late. *But*, thought Mick, *he'd never turned down a friend, hell for that mat-ter he'd never turned down a stranger….even if she wasn't completely human.*

It was the other thing in the room that troubled him. The eight-foot corn dolly with the skin of a smiley child's balloon stretched across its face (or whatever was underneath). It kept to the shadows and paid him scant attention and, for that, he was grateful. Alice Fiend described it as '*The Midwife*' and to Mick it seemed like a bit of a slow moving klutz, but he knew better.

Corn Dolly was made up of a thousand smaller beasts; revolting little parasites, each a foot long, blue with razor spikes protruding from their backs and hideously baby faced. He couldn't quite wrap his head around it all but Ms Fiend was adamant he'd always have a place by her side if he assisted her in her plans now. He would have wealth and immortality. Mick Jones would have it all. He noticed that Ms Fiend was still at the window; her volcanic hair a trail blaze down her back, that stare still burning out over the dirty, dusty little city.

Alice Fiend folded her arms and looked down at the little creatures from the third floor office of Blood Rag's headquarters. She'd scour this planet, rape it of every natural and synthetic resource and enslave those flesh wasters who referred to themselves as humanity. She'd obliterate those disgusting apes, it was self-defence, and to them she represented the oldest question in philosophy: Evil. It made her laugh, the acts she'd seen, the aspects of human activity she had been a witness to over the years. Humanity was a malignant force in itself, existing in its own right. She would take this world by force. She stood and stared and thought about the day *The Sisters* would fall from the sky. It made her smile.

4
Shivers

Bunny Flask had fallen through her apartment door well into the early hours of the morning, completely rubbered and screaming obscenities at her boyfriend Josh, who was sitting in the dark waiting for an explanation. Her head nattered away at her now like Courtney Love and her mouth tasted like a dog had taken a shit in it. She reached about and discovered she was alone in the bed. The heavy curtains were shut tightly, which she was grateful for. Tiny little scars of morning light moved across the wall. She rubbed the grit from her eyes and listened to the pitter-patter of rain on the window. Eventually she threw the blankets off and went in the living room. She was still wearing yesterday's clothes and a dry sheet of sick had run across her top.

'Hello,' she called out, walking into the room.

Josh had gone, leaving her greeting for Sissy Spacek, who glowered back at her from the poster on the wall above the television. She noticed that there was an envelope on the coffee table. Bunny picked it up and started reading.

Dearest Bunny,

I fear you have forsaken me for Blood Rag, I never did have the balls you did. I'll collect my 42 inch plasma.

When you're out...

Toodlepips Bunny

Josh

'**What a fucking** idiot!' she shrieked, tearing the letter up and tossing it out over her balcony.

Fuck him, fuck that fat boil Mick Jones and fuck Alice fucking Fiend. She made herself some coffee and turned on the news. More doomed tales; a blonde woman was talking in a robotic octave. Today a young man had been found cut up in Portobello, a young couple from the other side of the tracks had murdered and tortured their baby in a sort of ritualistic killing and Gardai were still searching for several missing women. Bunny switched to *The Alan K in the Morning Show*. He was interviewing Noir goddess Megan Abbott.

Fuck Josh, thought Bunny, feeling better knowing there were other people out there far worse off than her but guilty because she felt this way. She shivered; the skin crawled on her arms like a draught under loose carpeting. She rubbed them and decided that it could be worse, not knowing that, for her, it was only just beginning.

5
They Nest

Worms and parasites, dust and decay; Alice and Corn Dolly stood in the humid enclave of the *Doll House*. The walls swarmed electric blue with eager razor backs slugs. The seven women Jones had delivered to Alice were bound at the wrists and strung up with cast-iron chains. Some were in the later stages of the 'Caging'. Two of the seven were about to begin their wakes. Alice looked at the wretched creatures and noted that they'd all cocooned. Dolly had already flayed or was in the process of flaying the others. The skin of the victims stitched a macabre coat over Dolly's lumpy bulk.

'It's almost about that time Dolly Dearest' Alice smiled.

The eight foot creature towered over Alice and moved its head slowly up and down in acquiescence. Alice touched the cage, which was almost ready, and the protective film bit at her fingertips. The Doll House was a converted sauna in Jones's basement; the nest needed desert heat to sustain itself. For the time being she needed Jones more than he needed her. He was a seller, a buyer, traits she almost admired in the creature. She knew that time was at a premium and she needed to forage this city for as many soldiers as possible. The male of this species were obsolete when it came to breeding, it was the females she wanted.

'Alice,' came the limping, lisping wetness of Jones voice from behind them, sounding like a satchel full of furious snakes.

She hadn't heard Jones creep up on her and she was furious he'd even dare to come in here. The flesh on his face danced like a bad skin graft on a shop dummy.

'Don't,' she pointed a finger at him, 'you dare come in *here.*'

He backed away when Dolly moved towards him, grabbing the scythe she used for skinning off the wall.

'Dolly enough!' Alice clicked her fingers and Dolly stopped stock-still.

'I apologise for Dolly. She gets over excited, as you well know,' said Alice, throwing her eyes in the direction of the women.

Jones took out a handkerchief and wiped sweat off his brow. Alice shuddered. He really did disgust her and she looked forward to the time when she could make a recording of Dolly disembowelling him when she no longer required his services. She'd add it to her personal collection and call it '*Death and Ecstasy*'.

'Thought I'd come in, see how everythin' is, ya know?' he was sweating profusely now and breathing heavily, his hand adjusting his balls.

Alice glanced at Dolly, who was cradling the scythe like a mother would a child.

'Why?' she asked. 'You're not needed and, more importantly, *not* wanted here.'

'Now you listen here Missy, I'm the one…'

Alice shot one look in the fucktard's direction and his words were dead before they hit the floor. The more recent of the skinned was writhing about, trying to free herself; the viscera had already begun to harden and pitiful whimpers came out of her mouth. The matured cages began thrashing on their hooks. They looked like a human would if you filled their bodies with fat, the skin stretched obscenely into viciously distorted balloons, giving the parasite time to absorb the victim and duplicate an identical copy. One cage split and Alice turned to Jones.

'Out,' she screamed, showing the man the palm of her hand.

Jones needed no further instructions. He turned on his heel and fled. The creature clawed its way through twisted bone and rotting viscera and finally broke the protective film. Alice once heard that they never quite recovered from the trauma of being born. She knew this as surely as she knew her own skin.

6
Female Trouble

'**How did you** ever let that fat motherfucker bastard put his dick up you, whore?' Bunny asked Kiffany Boston-Gifford, taking a mouthful of her Long Island ice tea.

'I hadn't a shackle when I met him sweet. It was better than the beat' she clicked her fingers together in front of her face and sipped her sauvignon Blanc.

They were sitting in a popular gay bar on Capal Street called *Pantibar*. The owner was a notoriously fabulous drag queen, or so Kiffany informed Bunny. Bunny couldn't help but notice that she was just a little bit distant but Kiffany wasn't the kind of woman who did distant; she was always clawing her way into the very centre of attention.

'He sacked me for some cunt he just met. Mind you he is a sadistic fat fucker.'

An embittered husk of a man was eyeballing them from the bar; a crustacean eroded by the four D's – disease, disfigurement, destruction and decay.

'Hmm...' replied Kiffany, from a hundred miles away.

Thinking it wise to change the subject and seeing that

Kiffany was seven shades darker than the last time she spoke to her, Bunny asked, 'Have you been on the sun beds a lot?'

Kiffany's eyes widened and her mouth hung open so Bunny continued, 'Its just that those things can give you melanoma.'

Kiffany slowly let out a breath she'd been holding before saying, 'So what? At least when I do die of cancer my skin pigmentation will match the coffin my mother has selected for me.'

She snapped her fingers and nearly drained half her glass. Honestly, Bunny didn't know why she tolerated walking on eggshells for people sometimes.

The bar was nice, thought Bunny. Little lace knickers hung from soft lighting. It was a mix of antiquey velvet drapes and Warhol postmodernisty design with pictures of Dolly Parton on the wall, Brazilian bartenders mixing cocktails and a little black and white Jack Russell called Penny Dreadful running up and down the bar area.

'What happened with Josh?' asked Kiffany.

'Shit stick lied,' Bunny began, and added 'well Jones sort of rang Josh and told him I had a *problem.*'

Kiffany raised an eyebrow. Bunny knocked back the dregs of her Long Island.

'What sort of problem sweet?' Kiffany poked Bunny.

'With drugs Kiffany!' Bunny shouted.

Kiffany nearly took Bunny's eye out of her socket when she whipped her head from side to side to make sure nobody was listening in to their conversation.

'Keep schtum. I don't wanna be barred,' Kiffany slapped Bunny's bare arm, which stung like the bite of a silver fanged cocksucker.

Bunny rubbed it. She looked over at Kiffany, all T and A, but smart and funny too. She was intelligent and loved what she did. Bunny slyly watched the curvaceous strawberry blonde dream and wondered how she could ever have let that creeping dread Jones share her bed, let alone suck his knobbly micky? It must've been for the cash. If it was one thing Jones had it was money and power, and plenty of it, so how was an unemployed cult journalist like Bunny Flask ever gonna get comeuppance? What was she even thinking of vengeance for anyway? Nobody would be actually cutting her cheques from now on. Dublin was becoming like Paraguay. She was just waiting to see the breadlines start up and she'd be first in the queue.

'I'm gonna get that sonovabitch Kiffany,' Bunny said, after a few more mouthfuls, meaning every word.

Bunny glanced out onto the street, the evening held the promise of a bitter night.

'That sneaking conniving little abortion,' she hissed.

Kiffany was quiet for a while before she said anything.

'Yes, you are and I know exactly how we're gonna do it sweet.'

'We?' asked Bunny.

Kiffany looked straight into Bunny's green eyes and said, 'You know I love to explore death and pain; it makes my life so much more valuable!'

7

Razor Blade Smile

By closing time the evening's promise of a bitter night had made good – Dublin was miserable with rain. Bunny Flask watched her fellow drinkers ducking into abandoned doorways and nightclubs for shelter against the onslaught of wind and rain. Knowing there wasn't time to linger there Bunny practically threw herself in front of a taxi. Getting in she told the driver to take her to her father's place in Dun Laoighaire. The driver took a circuitous route and the road leading to her father's was paved with squat forlorn cottages, decaying industrial estates and miles of high-rise and council estates. As the cab navigated through the jumble of arterial roads, flyovers and property developments that ringed the city, the architecture morphed into decaying hotels overlooking the sea with small overgrown graveyards and pitch-black parks. The cab driver smiled at her with dirty eyes, spaniel jowls flapping and she returned his look with her finest razor blade smile. The taxi driver continued on, oblivious to the hate, which she could feel – and hear – throb inside her.

8
Bad Dreams

Bunny began that Saturday with a strange kind of quiet pain. There had been no dreams, just a never-ending nothingness which locked her down in a small room inside her own head amongst feverish shadows and the violent desperation of gagged memories like the spectres of still borns, screaming over and over and over. Grainy morning crept in and snatches of a song she remembered as a teenager came from somewhere, either above or beneath her.

Getting out of bed she stumbled, slamming her leg into a locker, and she bit down on her cheeks to stop herself screaming. She looked herself over in a tiny cracked mirror under the jaundiced hue of a bare bulb deciding, finally, that all things considered, she didn't look half bad. She routed beneath the kitchen sink and found a bottle of Diazepam. She dry swallowed four. She looked at herself in the mirror and whispered '*you're all by yourself*' and wondered if this was what other people called living?

Bunny sat on the toilet and felt all the shadows in the small box crouch about her, mocking, like the gawky old

cunts from the estate outside. She could hear Jones laugh,
mock and taunt her incessantly. The voices of every person
who had ever shit on her, ripped her off or violated her in one
way or another came crushing down on her – Jones, Josh,
Alice Fiend, her parents. She turned on the shower and taps
until steam filled the small room, blinding her to her own
bruising. She removed her clothes and forced herself under
scalding water and screamed hard, expelling the rage that
was burning up through her. The rusty water was the colour
of spoilt fruit. She slapped and punched at the tiles, the water
searing her skin, and carried on until she passed out.

9
Near Dark

Jones sat and watched and waited for a woman to approach his table outside the Fisherman's Bar on Bolton Street. This was where he normally picked up women so strung out, or desperate, or plain lonely enough they'd do just about anything for money. The sky hung low, the reluctant purple of a fading bruise, and he sighed. A group of boys with bum fluff on their faces, wearing trackie bottoms and passing around a bottle of Buckfast, surreptitiously shot glances in his direction. He drank his whiskey in one gulp, went into the bar and ordered another.

When he sat back outside a wretched creature with manky bleached yellow hair, viciously pulled back in a ponytail off her blotchy face smiled at him with crooked teeth. He gave her the once over; she wasn't ideal but she'd do. He had no sooner smiled back than she made her way across to his table. He noticed she wore no bra under her vest top and he could see the outline of her saggy tits.

'Ah roight mate, don' min if I join ya?' she pointed to the seat opposite him.

'By all means, be my guest,' he replied.

She slumped down in the seat, putting a bottle of Bulmer's on the table in front of her. Without a glass, he noticed. She bit at her fingernails, suddenly coy before taking a mouthful from her bottle and belching quietly.

'Scuse me,' she laughed, covering her teeth with her fingers.

He forced himself to smile back. She really was a sorry little thing and, by the time he was done with her if all went to plan, she'd be even sorrier.

'Sos why'd ya come up here?' she asked.

'Gets me out of the house. Never know who I might meet.' he made his gaze level with hers.

She blushed and began playing with her ponytail.

'Ya married so,' she stated, in a matter-of-fact way.

'I was, but that is done with now' he replied.

She went a shade redder and took another drink of her cider.

'Whas your name so?' she asked, lighting up a John Player and taking puffs in speedy succession.

'Phillip Cotton, and you?'

She ran her tobacco stained fingers over her greasy yellow scalp and tightened her ponytail.

'Michelle's my name.'

'Well Michelle, how would you like to make some extra money?'

When he looked at the sky he noticed it was near dark.

10
Reanimate(her)

When Bunny woke up she was in a room that was huge, cavernous. The walls were stained from the sodium glare of the street lamps, shadows fell across the terraces outside, slivers of light fading from bitter orange to petrol blue. She could hear dogs bark, their legs moving quickly, chasing their own pathetic shadows away, away across the estate. When she tried to breath it sounded like she was gurgling sand, she moved her arm from under her belly and almost screamed when she felt the reanimation of a million pins and needles. She vaguely remembered waking up in her father's, taking some sedatives, and getting into the shower.

Bunny listened and she could hear her dad downstairs in the kitchen beneath her bedroom pottering about. *How long had she lain here?* she wondered getting up from the floor and sitting on her bed. She poured the contents of her bag onto the quilt and looked through it all, not sure of exactly what it was she was looking for. That was when she spotted the keycard to Blood Rag HQ. The key she'd forgotten to give back to security on the day she was fired.

Her mobile was beeping and she saw she had a text message from Kiffany:

> how Ru sweet? Don't worry about any of this, I have things under control. Kiff x

After replying to Kiffany's text she looked out onto the street. The light was still deciding what colour it wanted to settle in. She'd dreamt of Josh. She stood watching young children argue over a makeshift trolley and tried to remember, but it was getting away from her. Each time she tried to capture the memory in her head it became fragmented, disjointed. She thought of her mother. Had she dreamt of her?

She stood at the window until the dream became dust. She hated that. It was a bit like life; you're always chasing an impression. One that gets weaker and weaker as the day moves sluggishly into night and eventually you relent and it's gone forever.

Bunny looked at the keycard in her hand. She'd go there and she'd wait for him tonight. She couldn't let this go. She would wait until dawn. With these thoughts she began to prepare.

11
Psycho

Jones brought Michelle to his estate near Mount Kippure. Ms Fiend and Dolly were at Blood Rag HQ preparing for the transmission of the signal. Michelle meandered dumbly about pointing at posters hung on the wall; he flinched every time her grubby fingers picked up an expensive ornament or ran her hand over a piece of furniture. Watching her he felt an irrational hatred, which wouldn't be satiated until he'd started hurting her.

She threw herself down on his expensive leather couch and asked if he '*had any booze*?' Without replying he went to the drinks cabinet, making sure he removed the bottle which was spiked with Rohypnol, and poured her a large measure. She nearly grabbed the drink from his hand and knocked it back, letting some of the alcohol spill over her chin. *What a revolting common little whore,* he thought. Jones carefully placed his own glass on the coffee table, smoothed his sparse oily hair back over his head and whispered.

'Come here, come over to papa.'

Michelle's eyes were becoming heavy-lidded and her lustreless skin was covered with a sheen of sweat. She pushed herself off the sofa but fell back when she tried to stand up.

'Was come ova me,' she said, wiping sweat off her forehead.

Jones removed a cut-throat razor from the inside pocket of his blazer. He didn't want her to pass out just yet. Her head hung between her legs and he gently ran his hand back over her scalp. She muttered something incoherent and his fingers slowly circled her ponytail. When he had a firm grip he yanked her head back as hard as he could. She screeched and he pulled her head back further, until he thought he could feel her spine creak. A wet stain appeared in the crotch of her trackie bottoms and she started retching. While her mouth was open he used the opportunity to grab her fat slug of a tongue and with one violent incision split the meat. She toppled off the couch and he held his nose with disgust when she voided her bowels. He stamped down hard on one of her hands and smiled at the satisfying crunch of her fingers snapping. Not long after she passed out he took her broken body down to the Doll House.

12
Hardware

Bunny sat at her kitchen table and tried to ignore her father muttering his disapproval at her choice of outfit under his breath. She took a mouthful of her coffee and, realising it was cold, went to heat the kettle up again. Her father gave her another one of his vicious looks and she knew he was about to go off on a vitriolic tangent.

'So what brought you out here anyway,' he began, 'dressed *that* way,' he asked, pointing at her outfit.

She watched the kettle boil and bit down hard on the inside of her cheeks.

'You can't come back here after everything and expect me to want to see you.'

His voice was starting to rise and it took every ounce of strength to stop her snapping his head off. She looked out at the garden shed and an idea began to percolate.

'Are you fucking listening to me?' he grabbed her, swung her around to face him and shouted this into her face.

'Yes,' she started coolly, 'I can hear every word daddy.'

The old bastard stood with both hands on the counter

with her in the middle, just looking into her face. *How could this man still scare her* she wondered?

'You,' he pointed, 'killed your mother being like *this*.'

She felt her heart drop. The kettle whistled, children screeched in the yard next door. Her father rested his head in his hands; how small he seemed right then, how very small and pathetic. She knew she felt anger, but it was a sort of muted anger, an anger her father wasn't even worthy of.

The kettle had boiled and she made another cup of coffee quietly, never taking her eyes off the garden shed, thinking of the hardware inside. It was completely dark outside; she was almost ready to go.

13
Sorry, Wrong Number

After four attempts to call Bunny's mobile Kiffany decided to try Josh's number instead. Her West Highland terrier Baby Sioux scurried around her apartment, banging into a table and nearly knocking the *GUTS* promotional chainsaw off her kitchen table. She was to cavort on stage with the chainsaw in a light pink dress at Dublin's Tripod nightclub later that month in the '*Devil's Cunt*' women only, horror festival. Cursing the silly mongrel, she hung up, poured herself a glass of wine and tried Bunny again.

Once again there was no answer so she left a voice-message. Resting the mobile between her elbow and her ear she eyed the packages on the kitchen counter. Just lying beneath was a poster of a dandy highwayman astride a skeletal black Bess; a popular young musician, who was rumoured to be a descendent of Dick Turpin. She paced back and forth and cursed Bunny, worrying the girl was about to do something impulsive. Kiffany knew you didn't do impulsive with Jones. She's seen, heard and cleaned up after him enough times to know that, whatever Bunny had planned, she was no match for him.

Kiffany had the tapes, pictures. Together they could force a confession out of him but, if Kiffany was entirely honest with herself, it wasn't a confession but hard cash she craved and the tapes were the only insurance she had. Jones frightened her and she already knew way too much about Alice Fiend and her plans already. She'd never have believed any of it in a billion years had she not 'accidentally' gone out there and seen those weird butterfly cocoons in the sauna. If only Bunny would let herself be reached.

'Girl, give her a chance,' Kiffany whispered to the dandy highwayman.

She called once more.

'Bunny! It's Kiffany. I hope you haven't decided to do anything without me sweet. Call me when you get this A.S.A.P,' and she hung up, hoping Bunny hadn't gone ahead and done anything already.

14
Bad Girls Go to Hell

Bunny slammed her father's door on the way out of the house. Throwing the bag over her shoulder she made her way across the cement garden that was her housing estate. She walked under a cloudy storm laden sky towards the DART, gazing up at now and again and checking the backpack to see if anything had fallen out. It was a soggy day, Séance weather, as Morticia Addams might say. When she was on the main street she was caught in a vicious tropical storm and had to run the rest of the way to the train. She started running, the skinny contours of other people's shadows passing her in a frenzied blur.

When Bunny reached the station she had to wait another fifteen minutes for the train to arrive. By that time she was as wet as she was on the day she was pulled out of her mother's womb. She checked her phone; there were five missed calls from Kiffany. Standing under the seething rain, she thought about her '*disorder*'. She thought about hope and, for some reason, imagined herself as an explorer lost in a desert. Hope was always for her a sort of mirage that ran away the closer she got to it, like a rainbow retreating into the horizon.

She wondered how people got thrown into these lives. How they were made to lead them whether they wanted to or not and, paradoxically, they'd often rather live than not. No matter what people were expected to endure – that world just out there was lonely and cold and brutal – but people'd always rather, above all else, be hopelessly alive. She was on her way to Hell and it didn't even bother her. The train had arrived.

15
The Substrate

Alice and Dolly stood outside the transmitting station on the top floor of Blood Rag HQ. Jones was out procuring another flesh sack for hosting so it gave them all the time in the world to awake the *Substrate*. This was the easiest way Ms Fiend could *'infiltrate the heads of their readership'*. Once the Substrate was activated, the frequency would go out and these wretched flesh sacks would be blind to the approaching Sisters who, at this very moment, were waiting at *Port Four*. Waiting for the *'Unicorn'* to open the inter-dimensional gate.

Dolly had slipped her skin – how Cthulu she looked, roaming about the HQ, exploring the Blood Rag roof. A vestigial creature; on her home world these creatures were farmed, sometimes for the express purpose of the infestation of other worlds, other times for sustenance. At its centre it had a simian face, with several tentacles, each containing four bulbs or parasites.

Alice moved the skin aside, strolling towards the window; it looked like Ramsey Campbell's Doll had eaten its mother. She leaned on the windowsill and looked down onto the rain soaked street and spotted a young woman crossing at the traffic lights. She was wondering where she'd seen her before when she realised it was the woman Jones had spoken of; that Bunny Flask! Ms Fiend continued looking down at her approaching and was struck by the realisation that this woman was somehow different to the other flesh sacks.

16
Give it your best Siousxie Sioux!

It took four attempts for Bunny's key card to grant her access to the HQ. The foyer was empty, which was odd; there was normally a security guard present at all times. Unnerved she went to the elevator, punched in the security numbers and made her way alone up to the offices.

'She's eager,' Alice smiled.

'Now,' she continued, looking sharply at the creature moving over the ceiling, 'Skin up Dolly.'

The creature moved with a certain graceful fluidity, not unlike some deep sea creature. Alice removed the Unicorn key from the transmitter and placed it on her desk.

Bunny leaned against the railing in the elevator. She was surrounded by Vince Ray style fetish posters, which hadn't been there when she was chucked out on her ass. It was obvious that this Fiend woman didn't know the first thing about working in the horror industry. She probably didn't even have a subscription to Netflix; seventy five percent of the films Bunny rented from there were horror. While the elevator made its way slowly up to the top floor, Bunny's anger blossomed violently. She'd dragged this magazine up by the grass roots and she wasn't about to just hand it over to Alice.

Alice ordered Dolly to get in a corner. She could play the prop while Ms Fiend figured out a suitable way to deal with Ms Flask. Dolly positioned herself beside the *'Clown'* prop and Alice decided to hide, wait and watch to see what Flask was planning on doing.

The elevator opened into a deserted office. The lights were still on and two new horror props had been placed by Bunny's old desk. A clown, 'how fucking original,' muttered Bunny, and something which looked like a hybrid creation of a creature from *The Gospel Singer* and *The Texas Chainsaw Massacre.*

Where was Jones though? wondered Bunny, before she noticed the Unicorn device sitting on her old desk. Bunny put the satchel down and picked it up. She thought she caught a movement in the corner of her eye but she ignored it and examined the Unicorn. What in the hell was it?

'Put that down right now,' came a voice from behind Bunny.

Bunny turned to face the woman who had taken Blood Rag away from her. Flame red hair, morgue pale skin; more brute than bitch.

'I take it you must be Alice Fiend?' asked Bunny, taking a step forward.

Again she imagined something move just outside her peripheral vision but didn't dare take her eyes off the woman. Alice stood defiant, arms folded across her chest, a smile flickering on her lips.

'Why are you even here? Jones told me he'd got rid.'

Alice didn't think this woman posed any kind of threat but, still, perhaps she'd make a good soldier.

'Not quite,' retorted Bunny and, taking two steps back, she picked up her satchel with one hand while holding onto the Unicorn device with the other.

Alice noticed this and hissed, 'I *really* do think it best that you put that down.'

Bunny laughed.

'Why? It's only a stupid prop.'

'Don't look now Bunny, but I think they might have a thing or two to say about that,' she laughed hysterically, and Bunny turned just in time to see one of the things she initially believed to be a prop come at her.

'Now,' hissed Fiend, 'lets see what you're made of.'

Bunny was overwhelmed and stood dumbly, staring at the shuddering creature looking down at her. *It looked like a scarecrow dressed as a midwife,* she thought. There was a noise like burning kittens coming from beneath the creature's skin, getting louder as it approached her. It was like the subdued yelping of a million depraved cherubs. Bunny swallowed sick when she spotted a bridal trail of decayed meat and maggots behind the creature. She looked at Alice and then back to Dolly.

Bunny gripped the back of her old desk and with every ounce of strength turned it over. Glass, sparks and smashing equipment gave Bunny a momentary respite but her gut told her that wouldn't stop this. Grabbing the pure alcohol she'd taken from her father's shed, she held her arm back and threw it. The impact shattered the bottle, dousing the creature. Bunny produced a match and, with a smile, threw it at her alcohol sodden would-be-attacker. Bunny heard Fiend scream. The fire was wild and vicious and Dolly danced and the bulbs screamed as the fire tore the creature apart bit by bit.

'Bitch,' Bunny turned to a furious Alice, 'should I toss this in too?'

Bunny brandished the Unicorn device in Alice's face. Alice gave Bunny a grin like a lunatic and replied, 'So come on then you little *slut*. Give it your best Siousxie Sioux.'

Bunny went at Alice like Buffy, Xena and Sydney Bristow combined. Alice's arm swung out, cracking against the side of Bunny's head... Bunny was unconscious before she hit the floor. Alice had the clown remove one of the barely alive bulbs from Dolly's remains.

'Get her knickers off,' Alice instructed it and, when the clown did this, Alice gasped at what she saw between Bunny's legs.

The bitch was a boy. Alice should've guessed right away. She knew what had been bugging her earlier: Bunny reminded her of the old school horror movie queen, Linnea Quigley.

17
Fuck Me Gently With a Chainsaw

Kiffany Boston-Gifford was parked opposite Blood Rag HQ when she saw what looked like a small explosion in either the central office or the boardroom. It was followed moments later by feral screams. Right at that moment, and entirely subconsciously, Kiffany reached into the back seat of her mini and retrieved the chainsaw. Kiffany was by no means a melodramatic woman but she knew someone was giving it to Bunny large and nasty up there in the offices and she didn't want to go in empty handed.

Unable to gain access to the building without a security card and not wanting to risk using the chainsaw in a residential area, Kiffany was left with no option but to go back and remove a tyre iron from the boot of her car. She would need to smash her way in. Once back outside, Kiffany closed her eyes, recited a silent prayer to her idol Maila Nurmi. She was certain the sound of smashing glass would be muffled due to Blood Rag being dwarfed by tenement apartments. She covered her eyes and swung the tyre iron.

*

Fiend held the squirming bulb close to her face. Bunny was perplexed by the tenderness Alice expressed to what appeared to be some kind of amphibious razorback with baby features. Her mouth was full of the metallic taste of hot blood and she was about to exploit Alice's distraction when the clown she'd completely forgotten about hauled her to her feet. Alice smiled and approached Bunny, extending the arm holding the razor back creature, when they heard the sound of glass breaking somewhere below them.

Kiffany took each step two at a time but she too noticed the new posters which lined the walls in the stairwell. Fucking Jones and the Bitch behind the Veil had replaced the selection of vintage mondo posters she and Bunny had selected with image after image of actress and actory morons. Could they spell *Red Porno*? wondered Kiffany.

It's all tits and ass, not talent and ability, which was what Blood Rag was supposed to be about. She pondered while making her ascent how a nubile young woman's flesh could be used as a sort of brainwashing tool, as if the pouting, lippy, titty, tanned images were calculated in some subliminal way. These tarts were in no peer group that either she or Ms Flask belonged to. They watched her climb, telling her and every other woman who was shoved outside of their spectrum *accept your place and never rise above it*. She'd reached the top of the stairs.

'I know my fucking place' she whispered before shouting, 'You can fuck me gently with a chainsaw.'

A shout that was quickly drowned out by the scream of her darling chainsaw.

18
The Phantom Broadcaster

It was only by chance that Jones heard the broadcast; a broadcast with a voice like crushed glass. Jones would sometimes lie awake late at night and let the voices from the radio soothe him. He'd never been a great sleeper. As a kid in Ballyfermot he had to share a room with his sister, Myra. She'd been dead for nearly twenty years now; ovarian cancer. He remembered the last time he had seen her, in the back room of his dead mother's house, a twisted thing carved by an agonisingly slow disease.

Sometimes he thought he could still smell her – the stale urine, and the meaty stench of her sweat – late at night when he was alone with only the voices floating in the air for company. This was when he heard the voice he came to describe as '*The Phantom Broadcaster*'. By chance he had heard this broadcast from a station, which didn't identify itself; he thought it was a rogue pirate station. Some student with too much time on his hands who talked in a loop about things that, at first, seemed unrelated to each other. But, when Jones listened closely, he realised this Phantom somehow knew about Alice's plans, or knew parts of them. Jones kept it from Alice. He didn't exactly trust her and she barely disguised her contempt for him.

From his bedroom window, his view of the sky hung low and red like a slashed throat. He decided he'd keep *The Phantom Broadcaster* to himself. He never was one to put all his cards on the table in one go and this way, if Alice did decide he was no longer useful, he'd have some ammunition against her. He lay in the dark and he listened and tried to discern the secrets between the words. Of course, this wasn't the only card Jones had up his sleeves and, when he saw the lights of the van, he knew she had finally arrived.

19

The Sky is Full of Dead Worlds

The fingers of the clown's grip were steadfast and Fiend held the razorback inches from Bunny's face. The razorback's mouth was lined with two rows of translucent blue daggers and these nasty little diamond spikes were eager to sink into her face unless she did something quick. She kicked out and her foot met Fiend's stomach knocking her onto her ass. Alice dropped the Bulb, which squirmed along the floor towards Bunny. Alice threw a stripe of violent red hair off her face, quickly regaining her footing. Despite the deadlock of the clown's hands and the likelihood that Bunny was about to die, she smiled. A smile she'd occasionally used on Josh, smug and hilarious and infuriating.

'That's right' she said to Alice, 'I am a boy, and I hit like one too. So you can chew on a shit-filled cupcake for all I care, you worthless cunt.'

Alice punched Bunny viciously in the face, snapping her head to the side. She stumbled. The clown's grip loosened and she elbowed it with as much force as she could muster. The clown hit the floor and Bunny twisted herself round to the exit. The door was locked, the clown was behind her and Alice blocked her way. If Bunny had known earlier she was about to walk into an Asimov short story, she'd have paid someone else to burn the office down but, if she had to she'd take this cunt down with her.

'So?' Alice asked, eyebrow raised, arms folded, her turn to be smug.

'I know I should of asked earlier…' but before Bunny finished the sentence, the scream of a chainsaw cut through the air and the door behind Alice exploded into a billion pieces of wood. Bunny, taking her chance, grabbed the Unicorn device from Alice's grasp.

Kiffany Boston-Gifford kicked the remaining wood through. She smiled at Bunny. Alice didn't dare take her eyes off Kiffany. Bunny calmly asked Alice again what she had been doing earlier.

'So?' asked Bunny, holding the Unicorn between her thumb and index finger, dangling it in front of her.

Kiffany powered down the chainsaw.

'It's for a frequency. Seriously, you wouldn't understand,' Alice replied.

'What *kind* of frequency sweet?' asked Kiffany, standing a few feet behind them.

'Was I speaking to you Kiffany?' replied Alice.

Confusion and the ache in her jaw stiffened Bunny's face. How did they know each other? Kiffany took two steps towards Alice. She had her hand on the string and was ready to pull.

'Wait Kiffany, what the fuck…' Bunny shouted, stepping in between the two of them.

'You hardly think that will stop me' asked Alice, pointing at the chainsaw.

'No,' Kiffany said, 'but it'll slow you down if you're not exactly, oh how should I say? In one piece.'

'Enough alright' Bunny screamed, shaking her hands either side of her.

She turned and looked directly at Alice Fiend. The woman showed no signs of retaliating. She regarded Kiffany only with a weary contempt.

'What is the frequency for, what does it do?' Bunny asked, rubbing her swollen jaw.

Alice walked to the window and stared at the sky.

'You think the threat is from up there Ms Flask, but it isn't. The Substrate is what the frequency will wake up.'

Bunny leaned against the windowsill.

'The Substrate?' she asked, looking into the other woman's face.

Kiffany put her chainsaw on the floor and interrupted them.

'Alice, tell Bunny about the ports.'

Fiend turned to Kiffany and Bunny thought, for a second, she was about to vault right at her.

'The ports are only islands, the surviving parts of my own world. We need the Unicorn key to open the gate and my sisters will fall. There is no point in trying to stop it. The Substrate *is* humanity.'

Still confused Bunny said, 'But won't those aliens want to take over?'

Alice smiled and then held her head in her hands.

'Yes Ms Flask, my home world is dying so I need you people for food,' Alice laughed and continued, 'I'm not a cliché; you think I'm using the plot of a bad pulp novella as my master plan?'

'Maybe,' Bunny replied, feeling like a shitstick.

'You,' Alice said pointing at them both 'are the aliens.'

'What?' Kiffany and Bunny asked together.

Alice folded her arms again and said, 'The Psyche is a feminine entity. Only the men will become obsolete my dears. It is *they* who are convinced aliens are up there, cowering in a sky full of dead worlds.'

'I hear you,' chirped Kiffany, kicking the clown in the ribs before it got back onto its feet.

Bunny stayed quiet. After all, this woman had been trying to kill her when Kiffany conveniently showed up. She looked at Kiffany, who had the toe of her shoe on the clown's throat, pinning him to the ground and then back at Fiend. Alice's face was a mask she had no way of reading and a part of her was grateful for this.

20
Terminal Island

The bulbs had been a crude route to the Substrate and, so far, Alice had nearly two hundred and seventy followers on this island alone. Bunny was sitting on the other side of the office, leaning back on a chair and wringing her hands. She still had the Unicorn key and Alice didn't want to force it from her, unless she absolutely needed to. Looking at her, Alice could never have guessed her biological sex. Her birth sex didn't matter. The Substrate would activate slowly with her, but it *would* activate. If she allied with these two, she'd no longer need Jones and this alone made her laugh inside.

The males would be processed and filleted. She wondered though, what Kiffany and Bunny would say about that? They hadn't agreed to an alliance yet and time was running out. She needed to open the ports soon. She approached Bunny and sat down beside her.

'I was once like you' she said quietly.

'You had a cock?' asked Bunny, sighing.

Alice laughed. *How had she come to this,* Bunny

wondered? All she wanted was for her existence to be one long John Waters style party.

'No, but I did have my head held under water while the rest of the world flourished'

'I don't trust you Fiend. You took this, Blood Rag, away from me.'

Bunny felt her voice about to break but reined it in just in time. Alice stared into the middle distance and said nothing for a long time.

'That was Jones Bunny, not me,' she replied eventually.

'What about trying to kill me with that slug?' asked Bunny.

'It's called a Bulb. That's what they are before they cage and become *Dolls*.'

Bunny rolled her eyes; this woman was a fucking nut. Bunny was sweating and she stank. The small office was boiling. Alice stood up and paced back and forth. It made Bunny uncomfortable.

'You killed Dolly. Self preservation is *paramount*. Do you get that at all?'

Sick of the cryptic shit this woman was saying, Bunny pushed her way past her. Kiffany had gone back to her car and the clown was back standing in the corner.

Seagulls circled in the sky outside like psychotic marionettes. Pools of tired rain made shapes like small islands on the panes of glass. *Like terminal islands*, thought Bunny. She turned back to Alice. What if Bunny decided to play along? At least until she found she had some more information, some leverage.

'You willing to come along then?' Alice asked.

'Well maybe I *will* and maybe I *won't*' Bunny replied, doing her best impersonation of the drag queen from *Vegas in Space*.

Alice's face softened, she picked up the transmitter before she said, 'You'll change, you need to know that.'

Bunny already knew all there was to know about the arduous, painful process of reinvention; or at least that was what she believed right then.

21
Angels are Devils

Here was a woman offering Bunny her hand and yet she was reluctant. The entire situation was more surreal than *The League of Gentlemen, Monty Python, Salvador Dali and Marcel Duchamp* put together. Who was Alice Fiend? Or rather *what* was she? Bunny felt inexorably drawn to this person even though, only hours earlier, she had tried to kill her. There was a witchy sort of otherness about her. She was an outsider, a deviant, a freak.

Bunny had been born mutilated by her own masculinity; this woman had been mutilated in her own special way. This woman was like her. Both of them wanted to transcend their own skins, punch, kick and cut their way through the membranous flesh of the chrysalis.

What happens then? Earlier Alice had said something about how men would become obsolete, did they face extinction? Could she stand by Alice and watch her herd the cattle? Had anyone stopped and helped when two teenagers on her own estate beat her so badly that she had to have her jaw wired? Had anyone stopped her mother doing what she did or stopped Bunny fucking men for money when she was 14 and still at school? Nobody had come to her rescue. Why should she help others? Bunny was like oil to other people; they slid away from her one way or another if they spent enough time hanging around her.

She'd only come here tonight to burn the office down, doing damage because she'd made this magazine, and instead, she'd found a strange kind of angel in Alice. But, Bunny realised, sometimes angels are devils. It wasn't just a few men Alice was talking about, it was every man. It was genocide.

Another thing that troubled Bunny was that Alice and Kiffany knew one another. Something too big to just slip Kiffany's mind. Kiffany knew more than she was letting on and Bunny would need to talk to her without raising suspicion. She didn't want to have all smoking guns turn in her direction. A question nagged Bunny though: could Kiffany Boston-Gifford be trusted?

Before she went any further she took Fiend's arm. Fiend looked at her, puzzled.

'What about Jones?' she asked.

'I'll leave *that* to you,' Alice scowled.

They made their way down to the street to where Kiffany leaned over the bonnet of her souped up car, chainsaw at her feet.

'About ready I see,' muttered Kiffany, getting in the car and not giving them a second glance.

22
Trauma

Sunglasses Steve had been keeping a check on Blood Rag since spotting the woman, who called herself Alice Fiend, in a soulless advertorial a month before. The advertorial was about a radio programme Alice was working on and Blood Rag had given out free gifts with Alice's introduction. He had known a girl a few years ago, went by the name Jessica Spark, that'd vanished. There was a terrorist attack in a small village – at least that was what the tabloids screamed - and he had been one of the only survivors, but her body was never found.

Sunglasses Steve knew that Alice and Jessica were the same person. He also knew that there had been no terrorist attack that day. He had seen the scarecrows. Seen the slaughter. Sunglasses had also witnessed what happened to Jessica at the barn. He had hidden for a whole day and snuck in when the scarecrows were preoccupied. She had been chained up, her body suspended so far in the air he couldn't reach to help. Now Steve could remember little more of what happened after that. He did remember it was a scalding summer and he remembered the screaming and the rancid air. This unsettled him more than the memory of staring into the dead eyes of the butchered.

It was like he had had one of those dreams. One too incomprehensible, too horrific, for a person to look at head on. It was always just a mocking, hectoring spectre stalking at the edge of awareness. So his mind created a veil and it never returned fully formed. It was a place always within him, but always outside of his reach. Whenever he left the house, which was rarely these days, Death wore the faces of everyone he saw; strangers he passed in the street, family, even his fuck buddy Danny was *different* somehow.

Jessica had mutated into some sort of chrysalis, skin like glass while something else formed underneath. Steve had somehow survived until the scarecrows left. But they'd been careless and left something behind. It was a peculiar device, like a mobile phone from 1998. Sunglasses Steve had called the *'Gemini'* because, carved on both the front and the back, were images of two strange creatures. It took him a further two years to learn how to work it. Once he did, he discovered a series of recordings. With this device Sunglasses had become 'The Phantom Broadcaster' Jones had heard.

With the *'Gemini'* he had learned of plans for the construction of underground facilities; a haven for the selected to hibernate on the day The Sisters fell from the sky. Sunglasses also knew that the only way to prevent this was to go to Mount Kippure, where the owner of *Blood Rag* Mick Jones resides, and wipe that Blood Rag bitch, and whatever cronies she'd accumulated, off the face of the earth. And he didn't give a fiddlers fuck about dirtying the face of his own humanity by doing so.

23
Meeting Death Along the Way

The car burned as it tore its way up the dirt path to Mount Kippure. Bunny sat in the back seat holding onto the Unicorn key while Alice sat with the transmitter on her lap. Every now and then she looked back at Bunny and smiled. They drove under a canopy in the forest, which made Bunny feel claustrophobic and the darkness in the mini made her queasy. Bunny thought of the last time she'd seen her mother before her death and what exactly she would do once she met Jones.

'Are you OK sweet?' Kiffany asked after they'd been driving for a good forty-five minutes.

'I will be, once we get there, Kiffany.'

Worry fell fleetingly across Kiffany's face with Bunny's words and she said no more after that.

Alice watched Bunny in the rear-view mirror. She was clinging on to the Unicorn. She wondered if the girl had it in her to kill Jones; she'd find a way to make sure she did it. For now she needed to save face and not take the Unicorn by force, but she was running out of time. The body she was in was failing her and she needed to open the ports and release The Sisters before she went to dust.

Kiffany screamed when the lights appeared from out of the dark; two beams of light, which cut bright like blade's through treacle. A Jeep was hurtling down the lane at a Holy Fucking Jesus speed, coming right at them. The lane was too narrow and there was no way they could avoid it.

Alice turned to the two of them and said, '*Laters*' before she kicked open the passenger door and threw herself from the mini. There were no doors in the back. Bunny was trapped. Before impact Kiffany decided to take her chances and, with a yank of the wheel, the car twisted violently to the right. The mini plummeted deep down into the dark mouth of a chasm in the forest. Bunny closed her eyes and all she could remember hearing was Kiffany scream, every pane of glass splintering and then coming down hard on her head. Her last thought before she was swallowed by pain and the night was *see you soon mother.*

24
Kissing the Wolf Goodbye

Before she took the name Bunny Flask after seeing a midnight screening of *Bunny Lake is Missing* in Portobello, Bunny Flask was a boy who went by the name, Adam Wolf. After leaving the morgue on the day of her mother's death, she noticed that the night had become just that little bit darker and she could still taste the strangers piss on her lips from the woods that day. Bunny had cut her mother off when she'd called the night before. She wanted to know where Adam Wolf was, why the Rivotril she hid under the sink was missing, who Bunny was with, what she was doing and with whom she was doing it.

His father had beaten Bunny that morning. The violence was nothing new; it had become a part of her over the years. She discovered there was nothing special or remarkable about it; it was something she had always carried inside her. She sought it out wherever she could find it. It was always available, if you knew where to look. Bunny always found bruising was fine but bleeding really impressed her and, from an early age, she had become accustomed to the reliability of pain.

So, she found it in the diseased cocks of strangers, in classified ads; she played the part of willing victim to perfection and was even something of a cliché. She kept razor blades in a shoebox under her bed.

When they found the remains of her mother, there was very little of the woman she knew left but this was a fact she'd grown accustomed to before her mother burned. They said she fell asleep while smoking in bed, which Bunny knew was a lie. The fumes of petrol lingered for weeks in that back room. Bunny knew her mother had carried it herself.

Her father blamed her for the way she dressed, for who she was, and Bunny was *never* a 'man'. She felt sick whenever anybody described her this way. She had already begun burying that part of herself a few months before her mother died. In a way her death let him go and she could finally kiss the wolf goodbye. On that day she cried for Adam Wolf and all the other girls forced to live as boys in the world.

25
Into the Womb of a Dead Woman

Jones had come to realise that there was real beauty out there – and not just in art, or music, or film, or the accomplishment of making Blood Rag the hottest horror magazine on the shelves. There was another sort of beauty. A way to transcend even the most exquisite things life had to offer and make them seem like dusty dull miasmas in comparison. He clung to this knowledge, this understanding engendered in him, because he had seen glimpses of it in the eyes of people driven deranged with fear, who he had been beaten to within an inch of their lives, pleading at his feet. He knew he was a sick son of a bitch and he didn't care. He'd watched his little sister shrivel and die, a disease dragging her away bit by bit into a terrible vacuum. Rationally, the man didn't believe in Hell, but he'd been there in nightmares, he could revisit it in those final moments of his sister's short life.

He heard it in the last frenzied screams of grown men before he kicked their teeth in or saw the reflection of a crowbar mirrored in their eyes before he let it fall hard on their skulls. For Jones such acts were not barbaric but transcendent.

*

The courier, a ratty man called Beaker, left the body outside the Doll House. His sister rotting; his dear Grim Little Myra, who he'd watched die in a pool of shit and puke and hopeless filth. He would finally have her back. He put on his finest suit for his finest hour at Mount Kippure. Mick Jones was going to put a bulb into the womb of a dead woman; his sister.

26
Bunny Flask is Missing

Bunny found herself moving, broken and alone on a dirt road and didn't know how she'd come here. She held something in her bloodied hand and knew she shouldn't let it go. All around her the myriad forms of night stalked and taunted her. The sky was slashed with pink and blue and mad birds were spinning like frightened tadpoles under frozen pond water above her, their cries cutting piercing her fatigue like a dish of ice water. She was bleeding and charges of pain ran through her arms and legs. It reminds her of when she was a boy.

Hands Tied to her feet while the red eye of a camera watches from the roof. The drapes on the window are heavy and nailed to the bare white wall. Two men the boy has met before have made him sit in a bathtub, tight rope cutting and turning both his hands blue. He is revelling in his own shit and piss. Other men are in the hallway, just outside the bathroom.

Bunny stumbled and her knees met the dirt, her free hand gripping soggy leaves, breathing a feeling like big hard hands slamming against her ribcage.

As a boy he is sitting alone in a room. Again the curtains are drawn and his only distraction is the intermittent ting of a smoke alarm from somewhere beyond the room. The bastard was there that day. He came into the room with the single bed, past the alarm clock and the Lydia Lunch posters.

The alarm screamed and he was shouting about his tools, His mother was shouting at the bastard. She had put the bastard's tools away safe. This didn't stop him twisting Adam's arm up behind his back until the bone made a weird noise.

'Whingey little queer,' the bastard shouted, slamming his face into the wall; the side of his face where his jaw had been broken.

'Good for nathin,' the bastard coughed and sputtered, 'bastard faggoty little lady.'

The bastard licked at his face and she laughed like a coy schoolgirl right behind him. The bastard pulled down his underpants, slowly pulled him back by the hair and slammed his face into the wall again. He winced more from the pressure of the wall than the pain. When the bastard pulled at him, he started to cry and she squealed, 'lil boy is havin' a laugh.'

The next day, the heat in that room became unbearable. The bastard had cracked his cheekbone again. When the bastard's hands roamed over the parts of his face that didn't protest in agonising pain, he thought it was a bit funny that his face was the shape of a pear.

They'd taken all his clothes. His tongue played with a tooth that was loose in the back of his head. The bastard had screamed at him, telling him he wasn't a girl while she had examined something in her hair, pinching it between her thumb and finger, her eyes crooked with concentration. So he stayed there with his pear shaped face and thought, I am a girl, always have been.

Bunny screamed 'no more' until the memory ran off like a wild dog. When she finally did stop, she thought her own screams were echoing back at her, until she realised that the sounds were coming from somewhere else.

27
Grim Myra

Jones hated it. Hated that thing he'd created in the Doll House. It couldn't be his sister; he believed she'd be like the others. Yes, he knew none had been dead when they were impregnated but each of them had been severely wounded. All of those had regenerated and became perfect replicas of the original. Although Myra was badly decomposed when he inserted the bulb, he didn't think this would be the outcome.

It glanced at him through the glass; it wasn't Myra or anything approximating her. This was a vicious sack of malevolence, as if insanity itself worked as a cancer eating away every nuance of personality, mental and physical. All that was left was a withered, battered string of meat with dusty sheets of skin barely coating a bitter, steel hard cage within. And, to Jones's utter horror, it continued to grow. It wouldn't stop growing. *This wasn't what she would have wanted,* he thought. This wasn't what he wanted at all.

Watching it glide around inside the Doll House he was overwhelmed by a succession of sensations. What could he do? Letting it out would be suicidal, it would rip him limb

from limb. *Could he burn the Doll House down* he wondered? Bring his Victorian pile down on top of it all? No,
that he couldn't do. He would leave it until dawn, just for
a few more hours, just for a few more hours. Just for a few
more hours…

28
A Lesson in Nihilism

Alice ran through the woods desperately wanting to get out of the dark and back on the streets. She could hear the strangled squawking of crows above her head, their beady black eyes searching for sustenance. The woods were the only thing she feared in this world; the woods and the magpies. She held the transmitter under her arm and kept moving, occasionally hitting the root of a tree and stumbling. She stopped when she heard a voice shouting 'no more' and, when she looked to her right, she saw there was a dirt path. A few yards down she could make out the silhouette of a young woman.

It was Bunny. She was alive and she was clinging onto something; she still had the Unicorn key. This time Alice would have to take it by any means necessary. She'd kill her if she needed to. There were other noises in the woods too though. She could hear screams further up the track; screams which sounded like an animal getting tortured. The noise gave Alice Fiend butterflies in her stomach.

She followed Bunny as the girl made her way towards the wounded. Let her be a nightingale if it made her happy. Alice quietly went in pursuit of the Unicorn key and Bunny Flask. She had to open the port to release The Sisters and release the *Psyche* soon.

Bunny staggered onwards, towards the screaming. It felt like she was clawing through the dark to reach whoever it was in trouble and she got the impression someone was watching her. Drops of water fell on her from the trees overhead and muck splashed all over her legs. She was sopping wet and freezing and desperately wanted a warm shower and a bed and a way out of this nightmare. What had she been thinking? Aliens, world domination, wakening the Substrate? She'd only wanted to burn Blood Rag down and now she had been catapulted into a substandard rehash of *Invasion of the Body Snatchers*.

It felt like she'd been walking for fifty years when she came to an overturned jeep. The cries she'd heard were coming from the man who was trapped under the wreckage. A part of her didn't want this. Why should she help this complete stranger? She firmly believed that other people should keep their pain to themselves. But an instinctual part of her was drawn to him. She had a similar feeling once when she heard a bird cry in agony and couldn't reach it. Her mind said one thing but her soul said another.

Bunny walked over to the jeep. The man was pinned down. Even if her mobile phone hadn't been smashed in the wreckage, phoning for help would be useless. She kneeled down beside him. He was a long-faced man with protruding eyes and a nose that had obviously been broken once or twice in the past. He looked up at her. She wondered if she could try and drag him out but, even though most of his lower body was covered, she knew he was a good two feet taller than her. Even if she did it would be like having a man-sized sack of spanners leaning on her shoulder.

'You'll be OK,' she said, and hated herself for sounding like an extra on *ER*.

She was just about to try for profound when Alice's boot slammed hard into the side of her head, knocking her face first into a pool of shitty, gore filled water.

Flecks of rain bit at the back of Bunny's neck as she pulled her head out of the water, pushing stinking, sewage smelling hair off her face. She felt like she was in the trenches, covered in blood and shit.

Alice snatched the Unicorn key out of her hand. Bunny watched her carefully. Alice had a large shard of glass in her other hand and was just about to use it when she was distracted by the croaking coming from the accident victim's jagged maw. Bunny searched the ground for something to defend herself with but was finding it more and more difficult with the lack of light and the rain washing the ground away.

Fiend strolled across and stood over the man. She carefully placed the transmitter and the Unicorn at her feet while bending down. Gripping the man's head on either side, she looked over at Bunny and smiled before twisting his head first one way and then the other. There was a sound of bones straining like chalk on a blackboard followed by a wet snap before Alice yanked the man's head from his body.

'Siser…his….sis...' the head mumbled, thick black blood running down over its chin; a tail of a spine dangling loosely beneath it.

Bunny retched, the taste of shitty water still in her mouth. Fiend kissed the severed head before hurling it into the darkness of the forest and turning her attentions back on Bunny. Bunny didn't want to die in this place; an empty wood full of ghosts. The kind of ghosts who never offer a reveal, but sneak up on you quietly, the sorts you at first believe are harmless.

Alice fiend was one of these monsters. She was no melancholy scrap of shadow but she was a creature that hid in dark corners, or under floorboards. Now here she was, creeping forward with a shard of glass in her hand, with every intention of cutting Bunny's throat. But then Bunny spotted the dark look in her eyes and the smirk on her lips and realised Alice wasn't going to use the glass on her throat. Bunny crawled backwards, the rain battering her face. With preternatural speed Fiend grabbed her ankle and pulled her back towards her.

'Alice, please, don't,' shrieked Bunny, kicking out and missing by a mile.

A vicious swipe of Alice's hand with the shard sliced through Bunny's cheek.

'Now Bunny, you're going to have a lesson in nihilism,' laughed Fiend.

29

Accentuating Their Dimensions with a Sawn Off Shotgun

Sunglasses Steve wouldn't have got past security to get into Blood Rag so he waited across the street straddling his Yamaha 96 with a sawn-off slung on his back and enough ammo to do her in his back pocket. He'd accentuate their dimensions all right, with his sawn-off shotgun. The first woman he spotted entering Blood Rag was a skinny pale little thing with jet black hair and a grungey dress-sense.

Not long after a mini trudged up the street at a slow pace and parked opposite. A blonde with big tits and a chainsaw galloped across the street when she heard a small explosion. She shook the glass doors and, unable to get inside, put the chainsaw down and went back to her car, returning moments later with a tyre iron and shattered the glass.

He waited and heard the chainsaw starting inside. He knew there was no security. He was about to treat the building like a lady and use the front entrance when the blonde came out like a whirlwind. Steve pushed his bike back into the shadows and watched her. She made a few phone calls, hung up and waited for the others who came out fifteen minutes later. *It was the skinny and*, he thought, *pretty brunette from earlier with the one at the very top of his cunt list; Jessica Spark.*

They talked amongst themselves for a while and he quickly started loading the shotgun with shells. He was about to take aim when he heard the mini speed away. They were away and safe from harm, for now at least. He started up the Yamaha and roared down the street, under an amber night sky.

Sunglasses tailed them, keeping as much distance as he could without making them aware of his presence. The rain and the fury of the wind didn't help and staying behind them was far more difficult them he could ever have imagined. Twice he lost, but quickly regained, control of his bike.

Somewhere near the turn off to Mount Kippure the mini disappeared and he came to the conclusion that it had gone off the main road. His suspicions were confirmed when he quickly turned into the dirt road leading to Mount Kippure. Even with the wind howling there was no mistaking the sound of brakes screeching, smashing glass and a furious crashing noise. He tried kick-starting his bike with no success. He removed the Gemini, hiding it inside his leather jacket. He walked steadily on, carrying the gun on his back all ready to smoke.

30

Men, Women and Chainsaws

Kiffany had crawled from the wreckage before Bunny had come round. Other than some surface wounds she was tickety boo. She hadn't wanted Bunny to go to Blood Rag and she had had every intention of protecting her girl from both Jones and Alice if she needed to but then, Bunny had been so easily seduced by Alice's preposterous lies that Kiffany felt no sympathy for her.

It was this alone that informed her decision to call Jones when she was outside the Blood Rag building and agree to a settlement in exchange for the blackmail material she had accumulated over the years. He'd told her to come to the house and they could come to some agreement. She didn't bargain on Bunny and Alice coming too. She was almost grateful for that car crash now. Bunny had dug her own grave, now she could lie in it. Kiffany was sick and tired of always putting on a face of exaggerated concern for the girl. She did like her but God could she grate.

Kiffany made her way up to the old four story house, which was a chapel Jones had converted in the early nineties at the bottom of Mount Kippure. Dim light burned in the window. She held on to her chainsaw and went down the steps leading into the old mortuary chapel.

When Jones had first taken her here she thought the building was a crypt or perhaps a folly, or even just a purely decorative structure. She opened the door into a small chapel, which still had an altar and pews. The place was used as a crematorium and it always gave Kiffany the heebies. Candles had been lit sometime during the night; most of them burned down to the wick. She checked her pocket and found a packet of *Pantibar* matches. She lit one and thought of her brother Keith. She missed home sometimes.

From somewhere overhead Kiffany could hear the faintest wailing, like listening to the world from under water. She exited the chapel and, one by one, took each step up and into the house, chainsaw prepped. A girl always needed something to fall back on after all, didn't she?

31
Psyche

Bunny had enough of her own damage to deal with without Alice adding another injury to the miserable play list of her life. She kicked, bit and thrashed but the woman couldn't be deterred. Alice's knee came down hard on Bunny's chest pinning her to the ground.

'Get off me you ugly bitch. I ought to punch your cunt in YOU RED WHORE!' shouted Bunny, grabbing Alice by the hair and ripping a clump from her scalp.

Alice swung round to face Bunny, teeth bared, and cracked her in the side of the head.

'Be patient boy. I'm getting there,' laughed Alice.

This incensed Bunny and she sank her teeth into Alice's ankle, biting hard and separating skin from bone. The fiend screamed and plunged the shard of glass into Bunny's thigh. Alice then reached up and ripped off Bunny's knickers and pulled her flaccid penis as far as she could possibly stretch it. Without looking at Bunny Alice remarked, as if she was about to sink a kitchen knife into a soufflé, 'Hmm. You're going to die a woman.'

Bunny couldn't manage another scream so she just stared at Alice. There was nothing more she could do, she was on her back, it was hopeless. She was about to be gutted like a spring lamb by a creature masquerading as the editor of a horror magazine. She steeled herself against the first cut when a voice came out of the rain behind her, and the voice had only one word to say, 'Jessica.'

Alice looked like a dog had just shit on her grave. She dropped the shard of glass, her lips slightly parted, and stood up slowly. Bunny hauled herself up off the ground, her body bent double with pain. A young man with a sleeveless leather jacket, sunglasses, floppy black hair which hung heavy with grease either side of his face, thick lips and a dirty tan stood a few feet away pointing a shotgun directly at them.

Bunny covered her cock with her bruised hands. Her face burned with shame. She thought that pointing a shotgun at Alice showed arrogance in his own ability. She also thought that he was something of a poseur but she'd still like to see him with his ass in the air. Ms Fiend stood watching, waiting for him to speak.

'I was at the scarecrow festival Jessica. I saw what happened. Remember?' Bunny was impressed; he said this without taking his eyes off Alice for a second.

'That was someone else, not me,' Alice replied, her voice full of ice and despair.

This unnerved Bunny more than the boy holding the big gun.

'I know about the Substrate and what it is going to do.'

Steve took a few steps forward. Alice didn't even flinch.

The sky was now the colour of wet cement, with sluggish trails of dirty black clouds.

'What exactly is the Substrate?' asked Bunny and they both looked at her.

'The *Substrate* is just a word Jessica picked out of a dictionary Mister,' said Steve.

'It's *Ms* actually,' replied Alice, breezily.

'Shut the fuck up you   alien whore!' he shouted, gun aimed between Alice's eyes.

'Sorry,' he said, looking at Bunny and meaning it.

Bunny suddenly felt even worse; covered in shit and blood with her cock in her hands.

Steve held the gun up to emphasise he meant business and started, 'All I know is that the Substrate is something *living* but dormant.' He lowered the shotgun and wiped the sweat from his forehead, which gave Alice all the time she needed. She quickly grabbed the transmitter and the Unicorn and escaped into the depth of the woods.

Steve fired some shots after her but only managed to hit a few trees.

'Fuck! Fuck! Fuck!' he screamed, close to tears.

Bunny wondered what he meant by *living but dormant* so asked.

'The Substrate is only a word she's used up till now. That device and transmitter will open a port' Sunglasses explained.

Bunny was having difficulty keeping up with him. He walked as he spoke.

'And what happens... Sorry what's your name by the way?' asked Bunny.

'Steve. You?' he smiled.

He had one of those faces which, at first, was nothing to sing home about but the more you looked at it the more beguiling it became.

'Bunny Flask,' she replied, holding out her hand.

Steve gripped her small hand in both of his and, if it hadn't been for the oestrogen, the grip of those large agricultural hands would have given her a semi.

'The Substrate is the machinery that underlies the mind, but the mind isn't confined within the head or the body,' he said, while staring into middle-distance.

Puzzled Bunny walked alongside him for a while trying to swallow what he was attempting to explain to her. She grabbed his arm and stopped him.

'Look, none of this makes any sense,' she felt her voice going up an octave.

'Basically four ports will open, The Sisters will be unleashed and *they* will be followed by something called Psyche. Psyche is a malevolent entity which will consume, control and eventually destroy anything and everything with a consciousness on Earth' he almost barked.

'But how is that connected to the Substrate?' Bunny asked sheepishly.

'Because Bunny,' he began, and took hold of her shoulders 'it will *wake* up something in us. Our minds will no longer be our own. It won't just wake the Substrate it'll infect it too.'

Bunny thought about pointing out that our minds aren't really our own anyway but then thought better of it. She felt like Clive Barker's heroine from The Great and Secret Show

Tesla Bombeck only, ironically, Tesla had bigger balls than Bunny.

'So we stop that happening?' she asked a question that went unanswered.

On both sides of her she could hear the wind bite and whistle through the woods. It was almost dawn now, she noticed.

'How do I know *you* can be trusted?' she asked, glancing at him, trying to figure out the colour of his eyes behind those ridiculous glasses.

'You can't, but lets just say its better that I'm on your side for the time being at least,' he replied and they walked on silently, making their way to the house at the bottom of Mount Kippure.

32
Slaughter! Slaughter!

Kiffany couldn't get much sense from Jones. He sat sobbing with the ball of his fist pushed into his mouth, sprawled across his couch stinking of alcohol. Whenever in doubt Kiffany decided the only solution to problem solving was a swift drink. She poured herself a large measure of rum and knocked it back while pouring another. She sat back down beside him.

His face was so distorted by misery that she thought he looked like a back-street abortion. She left him bawling for a few more minutes while she quietly sipped her drink. She looked across the room at an artist's rendition of herself, which was still hung over the fireplace. She liked the picture. It made her look like an insouciant French slut. She turned her attentions back to the heaving bulk shuddering on the sofa and wondered what she ever saw in him? He was only a step up from a German Shephard.

'What's the matter sweet?' she asked, laying a hand on his shoulder.

He violently pushed it away.

'Well that's fine, where is my money?' she demanded, arms folded across her breasts, a technique she often used when she wanted something she couldn't have. Kiffany was a girl who wouldn't take no for an answer.

Jones looked at her with eyes that had about as much life as road kill. A strange smirk replaced the tears on his ugly fat face. Kiffany was beginning to get really pissed at the motherfucker. She was wondering if Bunny had woken up yet. What if she'd been seriously wounded? She'd just left her there, in a mangled wreck, on a freezing night and for what, money? She was not a superstitious woman but even she thought that was so callous an act that it was likely to come back round and bitch-slap her someday. She was fond of Bunny, when she looked at Jones she knew that he was proof that there were some people in the world who deserved to die, but Bunny Flask wasn't one of them.

'I will only ask one more time, where is my…' but before she could finish the sentence she felt something sharp pinch hard between her shoulder blades and then Jones's face was covered in blood. When she looked down, a ghastly hand was holding her still thumping heart in the palm of its hand.

'Doom...' was Kiffany Boston-Gifford's final word.

Grim Myra had broken out of the Doll House. The thing stood looking down at Kiffany's eviscerated corpse before turning its attention back to Jones. To his utter horror it recognised him and wasn't attacking. Instead its long fingers began stroking the side of his face, the tongue like an eel licking its emaciated features lasciviously.

'Micheal,' it said clearly although, at first, he thought he only imagined this.

'Myra?' he whimpered.

'Yes, it's me. Why did you look for me?' it asked, and he didn't understand what it meant.

The stink was atrocious and the strings of skin, which hung down from it were coated in maggots. Other creatures he couldn't identify scurried and squirmed in its eye sockets.

'What have I done to you?' he whispered anxiously.

'Nothing worse than when I was breathing little brother,' it replied. 'Nothing bad at all.'

It stroked his face again. When it crouched down spreading its legs wide, his eyes strayed to the place between them. His mind no longer had any kind of purchase on a feasible reality. What he saw snatched the leftovers of his sanity away before Myra pushed his head between her legs.

33
The Invasion of the Dolls

The first thing Alice did once she reached Jones's house was to bring herself down to the Doll House. She would start the Doll's wakening earlier than expected and to hell with this planet. She'd made a grave mistake attempting to indoctrinate Bunny Flask. The girl was a gullible self-involved little prick.

When Alice came to the entrance of the Doll House she was surprised to see the door was open but, when she got closer, was shocked to see that the door had been forced open from the inside. It was dark when she entered and she slid on the floor. *Had the births already begun?* she wondered searching for the light. What confronted her when she switched it on enraged her.

Malformed Dolls crawled and slithered all over the floor of the sauna. Someone or something had ripped the Dolls from their cocoons and whatever was responsible had mutilated the defenceless creatures. Some had been hollowed out; lungs, intestines, hearts, bowels and wombs scattered everywhere. The ones that were still alive were failing quickly.

Alice Fiend felt fear circle her spine like a serpent. The thing, and of this fact she had no doubt, that did this was a creature she had no desire to meet. Jones must be responsible. She didn't give it anymore thought. It was time to open the port.

The Sisters would clean this mess up. She was alone, she was troubled by the thought, and she had sent the other Dolls out into the city. She closed her eyes. Dolls carried the imprint of ancestral memories buried deep in the Psyche. She reached out into the darkness of her mind and found The Sisters waiting. Comforted by this she readied herself for opening the port at the top of Mount Kippure.

34
Corpse Bitch

It was the screams of Jones that brought Bunny and Sunglasses into the dining room. Kiffany's chainsaw was over by the fireplace. It was definitely Jones grunting but neither of them could see what was happening. A large overturned couch was obscuring the view. Tentatively Bunny walked a few steps behind Sunglasses, who held the shotgun in front of him. When they finally could see what was happening Bunny held her hand over her mouth.

Kiffany's body lay cold and brutalised. Something long, thin and rotting was squatting over a naked Jones, who was screaming in agony because the creature had gouged his eyes out.

'Shoot it,' hissed Bunny quietly.

Steve didn't answer, just stood and stared. Bunny elbowed him hard in the ribs.

'Hey,' he shouted, rubbing his side.

The creature heard them and got to its feet. It was even more ghastly than the thing Bunny burned at the office. It looked like The Grim Reaper from *Cemetery Man*. Sunglasses aimed and fired, blowing a large chunk of its ribcage away.

'Now I must say, that wasn't a very nice thing to do,' the creature sighed, wagging its finger at them like a mother would a naughty child.

Sunglasses aimed the shotgun again and the creature charged. Bunny was knocked to the floor while this corpse bitch lifted Sunglasses off the ground. He still had a firm hold of the shotgun but hadn't enough room to fire. The corpse bitch sunk her nails into Sunglasses mid-riff, with every intention of splitting him open.

Jones crawled along the floor, a not quite slaughtered pig. Sunglasses punched the corpse bitch and his fist sunk into her rotting face. It stumbled away and Bunny grabbed a candelabra. She swung and it connected with the side of the corpse bitch's head. The creature staggered and Bunny did a one hundred and eighty degree spin, swinging it again as hard as she possibly could. This time she struck gold. The already fragile cranium caved in and the corpse bitch went down.

Sunglasses lay on the floor, a hand over his bleeding chest. The wounds weren't deep. His Sunglasses had been knocked from his face during the fight and Bunny could see that his eyes were a hard green. In the battle she had completely forgotten about Jones, until she heard him whining. She kissed Steve and went over to the fireplace and picked up the chainsaw. Jones was on all fours and she kicked him hard in the stomach, knocking him onto his back. He let out a pitiful cry.

'Don't bother begging,' said Bunny.

'Wait, Wait,' cried Jones, holding his hands in the air. 'Is that you Bunny?'

'It *is,*' she replied, coldly.

'Help me, please.'

So he did beg after all.

'Of course,' she said, and started the chainsaw.

Bunny had sometimes been the squeamish type but using a chainsaw on a human body was almost as easy as using a gun she imagined as she cut through pink skin, saggy muscle, putrid viscera and calcium deficient bone. Jones stayed alive a lot longer than she expected, screaming until he drowned in his own blood and vomit. Bunny relished every second of her gore opera. When she was done, she turned to Steve, who'd been sick all over the floor. She had a feeling he might be a lightweight.

'Now…' Bunny declared.

'You're ins…' he started, but stopped himself just in time.

'Now?' Steve asked nervously.

Bunny raised an eyebrow. '*Alice,* you plank,' she said, helping him up off the floor and added smiling, 'All things are possible boy.'

35
The Sister's Fall

Alice knew she would get there now. The end was in sight. The Sisters would arrive bringing Psyche with them. They would wake the Substrate; the mechanics beneath consciousness itself. Some would even describe the Substrate as the psychology of the universe. Psyche would possess it and this tiny world. She would pour into this universe as quickly and addictively as heroin running through a user's veins.

Alice looked at the pale orange sun hanging over a grey sea in the distance, and then down at a highway with ordinary people driving ordinary cars to their ordinary jobs. There was a small stretch with a lavender field beside a closed down factory, a garage and a small yellow pub stood opposite it. Old meadows and miles and miles of dirty white sky; a sky that would burn hot pink when The Sisters came through the port. She placed the Unicorn key into the transmitter and activated the frequency.

When Bunny and Sunglasses came out at the back of Jones's estate they discovered a small-log cabin with a garage beside it.

'We have very little time. There might be a car in it,' Bunny said, pointing at the garage.

'Wait,' Sunglasses Steve said, softly taking her arm.

He reached into his jacket and took out the Gemini, holding it in the air in front of her in the cold morning light. She knew by the expression on his face that he wasn't going any further.

'I'm not going back, even if you turn away,' she said, jabbing a finger into his chest.

He gave her the shotgun and she slung it over her shoulder.

'What is that anyway?' she asked, looking at the Gemini.

'It's how I got the information about Jessica and her plans; about the Psyche. But it's also a key. That other key Jessica has opens the ports right? Well this closes them...' his voice trailed off.

Bunny beamed at him.

'So it's *that* easy, all I have to do is use that and things will be back to the same as always. Right, gimme.'

'No, there's a catch you see,' he replied timidly, and she swore she could almost hear the fucking violins.

'Which is?' she asked, not really wanting to know the answer.

'This isn't *just* a key. It's a weapon. The explosion caused by using the Gemini to close the ports will destroy everything within a one-mile radius,' he said, quietly.

'You piece of shit,' she spat, slapping his face. 'You knew this and were never willing to do it? So instead I'm putting my tits on the line?'

'I just came for Jessica. I figured if I stopped her...'

'So I've to burn up there instead of you?' asked Bunny.

Steve just nodded, which made her feel even crazier. She held the gun under his chin. She never imagined her life having such a high body count.

'On the ground,' she ordered him.

Confusion spread across his face and his mouth hung open. She hit him with the butt of the gun, smashing his nose all over his face and knocking him down.

'Roll over, I don't want to look in your eyes when I do this,' she said sincerely.

He was dazed and sleepy looking but he lay down on his stomach without protesting. With the heel of her shoe pressed against the back of his neck she pushed his face into the dirt. She might have been half animal after everything she had been through; her mother's indifference, her father's drunken breath on her face, Jones cruel dismissal of her, being dumped by Josh and drawn into Alice's nefarious scheme. But she was still a woman and had some feelings left. If she looked him directly in the eye she might change her mind and she'd all but run out of second thoughts.

'I'd like to say I'm…' she couldn't finish the sentence or pull the trigger. *What a fucking anti-climax*, she thought. Steve carefully heaved himself off the ground. If all men were going to die anyway, maybe shooting him would spare him that suffering? She raised the gun again and his eyes widened in fear. She swung, bashing him in the side of the head. He fell to the ground unconscious.

'I'll just leave you to escape, if you have the strength.'

She went to the garage and tried to yank the door open. It was stuck and, even though she kicked that door like a harlot sitting on a hot-tin dildo, it wouldn't budge. Frustrated she sighed, kicked the door once more with no luck and then something caught her eye.

There was a sign she followed that read 'Sally' pointing to a field on her right where a working horse was chomping down stingers.

'Well hello there Sally,' she squealed, delightfully firing a shell at the sky.

The horse didn't even flinch and it took next to no time to mount that mare.

'Come on Sally...' she said, taking hold of its mane and kicking hard.

The horse reared up and almost knocked her off. She kicked the horse again and Sally galloped towards the hill; to the end of her world.

By now a cyclone was swirling above Mount Kippure; the highs and lows of air pressure systems being transformed into a fiery vortex which spit spider threads of venomous red and dirty orange out into the sky. It looked, thought Bunny, like the veins on a dead person's legs. Liquid blue fire crept down from a fissure in the sky and it appeared to be constructing some sort of machinery around The Unicorn. She'd need to act fast or she wouldn't be able to get inside.

Alice Fiend stood in the heart of the maelstrom, her head thrown back, arms stretched open wide. Bunny stalled the horse. There were only two shells left so she needed to make the shot count. She loaded, aimed and pulled the trigger. Alice's shoulder exploded in a supernova of gore and bone fragments but it seemed that the shot barely registered with the fiend. She looked in Bunny's direction, mild annoyance on her face. Her arm hung limp and broken at her side.

Bunny slung the gun back over her shoulder and charged. She would trample the bitch until she was nothing more than a stain smeared in the earth. Alice stood her ground while Sally came at her. When the horse was within spitting distance from where Alice stood, Bunny used the opportunity to throw herself free. She hit the ground and the Gemini was thrown from her hand. Sally hit Alice, the horse pulling the woman under and crushing her beneath its hooves.

When Bunny looked over Alice was getting back up. The bottom part of her jaw had been ripped from her face and her tongue wriggled about like a worm left to die in the sun. Alice and Bunny were now trapped. If either wanted to escape, they'd be forfeiting their lives within the electrical storm that opening the port had generated.

Alice was making her way slowly but surely towards Bunny. Bunny had one more shell. She was shaking so hard she wasn't sure if the barrel was aiming at Alice or not. Her vision was becoming impaired; a violent headache was hurtling in her direction. She remembered reading once that vision and migraines are intrinsically linked to storms. A fluorescent blur was gnawing away like a rabid cat at her corneas.   T h i s was her last chance. Alice was still coming at her. All Bunny could see now was little more than strips of colours circling the bitch. Her vision went from monochrome to lurid Technicolor until, without warning, it suddenly returned completely.

'I always thought I'd have something witty to say in an apocalyptic situation,' Bunny shouted, over the noise of the maelstrom.

She lowered the gun and blew Alice's leg off at the knee. If Alice could have, she would have howled. Instead she just went crashing down. Bunny grabbed the Gemini and ran as quickly as her weary body could carry her over to the transmitter.

The Unicorn key was sticking out of the top like a blade parting a veil. She glanced above her. The Sisters were already racing down through the tunnel. Bunny was astonished at how beautiful they looked, celestial even. She needed to close the port before the temptation to get a better look took hold of her sanity, or she'd be obliterated. Once they got past her, well she might not care that much about the rest of stinking humanity, but she sure as shit wasn't about to let these bastards lay waste to a world that might have beaten, raped and burned her, but nevertheless nurtured her in its own sick way to.

She was just about to use the Gemini to close the gate when Alice dived on her from behind. Bunny threw her head back. She felt Alice's nose crack. Alice clung on, fists beating down on Bunny's head, skin opening, more blood on her lips, in her eyes.

'Give it up Fiend,' she gurgled.

Bunny brought her foot down on the bitch's instep. Alice let go but not before Bunny had grabbed her hair with both hands, and pulled her over her shoulder. The Unicorn key tore a hole through Alice when she landed on it, nearly splitting her in two. She was stuck there, a dying pathetic thing.

Bunny bent over to look into Alice's eyes and, kneeling down, she gently pushed the hair from what was left of her face. She held up her hand, showing Alice the Gemini.

A single tear ran down the fiend's face. Tears welled up in Bunny's eyes too, but not for cutting Jones up, or for this bitch She was crying for the creature she'd somehow become since losing her job; or was this the woman she'd always been? Gullible, witless, impulsive, violent, and all because of this bitch in front of her.

Bunny might be dead soon too and Alice was well aware of this. Perhaps in her own warped mind Ms Fiend believed that it was a minor victory; bringing Bunny with her. Bunny leaned in closer.

'Take this you alien bitch,' whispered Bunny to Alice, before plunging the Gemini into her throat.

The fiend's body thrashed and shuddered and, a short time afterwards, she began to fade, the skin peeling off like old wallpaper, the bone softening, until Alice was blown away, bone by bone into the electrical field.

There was another keyhole where the Unicorn stood. Bunny took one more gaze up into Hell. The Sisters were closer and she could see them clearly. In another time folk might have called these creatures Angels. She knew no such thing existed. She placed the Gemini in the keyhole, looked back up at The Sisters and the burning sky and whispered, 'Let me die a woman...' before she closed the port.

The End